MURDER IN THE 1920S

A GREEN OAKS BOOKBINDING COZY MYSTERY BOOK 1

PENNY BROOKE

CHAPTER ONE

harlotte Young stared up at the crumbling manor with a heavy heart. The air was crisp around her, and she flexed her hands nervously. It had been years since she had been at her grandmother's house, and it felt strange being back after everything that had happened.

Her tortoiseshell cat, Archimedes, meowed insistently at her feet. He was a chubby rescue cat that she had gotten about a year before her grandmother died. Archimedes enjoyed three things in life: complaining, sleeping, and eating.

"Come here, you monster," Charlotte said, picking Archimedes up and rubbing his head gently.

He sneezed and glared at the house balefully. Her other feline, a sleek black cat named Roma, sat by her feet. Roma was younger than Archimedes, and had been rescued as a kitten. Sometime before moving to the small Massachusetts town, Charlotte had felt the need for another cat, and Roma had grown up in a small apartment with only Charlotte and Archimedes as companions.

Despite that, Roma was a friendly and adventurous cat who enjoyed spending time outside. She hadn't had much of a chance to explore the outside world when they lived in the city in Charlotte's tiny apartment on the fourth floor of a ten-story building.

When Charlotte received word that she had inherited her grandmother's old house, one of her first thoughts was that Roma would have an entire garden at her disposal.

Archimedes meowed again, likely wondering why they were standing out in the New England cold. Charlotte knew that all she had to do was walk up to the door and knock. She didn't have the keys yet, but she knew the housekeeper, Isla, would be inside. However, she wasn't quite ready to step over the threshold yet.

She had been close to her grandmother, and it felt wrong that she was moving into the house that her grandmother had lived in for most of her life. A part of her had wanted to sell the place and invest the money, but she knew it would have offended her grandmother.

Charlotte had spent every summer of her childhood visiting her grandmother, and she had fond memories of the manor. Besides, she worked from home now, and it would be an adventure.

"This was a good decision," Charlotte told herself softly.

She wasn't the adventurous type. Sometimes, her anxiety was so severe that she couldn't move her body. She had never been one to seek the company of others, and spending the better part of two years in a tiny apartment hadn't done anything to help her social anxiety.

Her therapist had encouraged her to take more risks, and what bigger risk was there than moving to a tiny town like Green Oaks and taking over her grandmother's old home?

"Maybe it was a mistake," Charlotte said, looking down at Roma, who was still grooming herself.

Charlotte had packed all of her things and sent it ahead with a moving truck. She had followed behind in her own car. Roma hadn't minded the car trip, but Archimedes had complained so much that she had to get pills from the vet to put him to sleep.

The front door opened, and Isla came bounding out. Isla was in her early forties and had started working for Charlotte's grandmother, Jenny, when Isla had finished high school. Isla had started out as a maid, but she'd managed to work her way up to become Jenny's house-keeper and financial manager.

"There you are!" Isla exclaimed, her face bright with happiness.

Isla was one of those people who made everyone around her feel wanted and loved. She had a warm, sunny disposition and a friendly face. Everyone in Green Oaks knew her, and it seemed like she was friends with someone. Greek Oaks was a small town with a population of fifteen thousand residents. Most people knew each other, but everyone knew Isla. She had grown up in the town and had never left, as far as Charlotte knew.

"How was your trip?" Isla asked, looping her arm through Charlotte's.

Isla was about ten years older than Charlotte, but she always felt like one of Charlotte's peers. The house-keeper looked younger than her years and gave off a youthful energy.

"It was fine," Charlotte admitted. "I thought it would never end, but now I'm here, and I have no idea what to do with myself."

Charlotte had to look down at Isla slightly as the housekeeper only just reached past Charlotte's shoulder. While Isla was petite, Charlotte was also uncommonly tall, reaching almost six feet. It used to bother her more when she was a kid, but she hardly thought about it anymore. Her height only became a problem when she tried to buy clothes since most pants and dresses were too short for her.

"I can just imagine how weird this must be for you," Isla said with a wince, "but I want you to know that Jenny loved you very much. She was worried that you wouldn't want to move all the way out here. I'm sure she would have been proud of you for making this decision. Come on, I set your old room up for you. If you want a different room…"

"My room is fine, thank you," Charlotte said.

Isla nodded sagely and led Charlotte up the stairs. The manor was an old Georgian Revival mansion that had been built in 1902 by Richard Stanhope, a mining magnate. He had chosen to move to Green Oaks since he'd owned a mine nearby, and he had claimed it was the most peaceful town in all of America.

The house was eventually sold to his son-in-law and was later passed down to other family members until it was sold to the Young family in the 1970s when Robert Young brought his new wife, Jenny Young, to town. Charlotte's mother had grown up in the manor, and the house should have gone to her. Sadly, her mother had died about ten years prior in a car crash.

It was part of the reason why Charlotte was reluctant to take up residence in the house.

The manor was still beautiful with two stories, fifteen rooms, and large marble columns in the front.

"I don't remember it looking this rundown," Charlotte admitted as they walked into the house.

The place smelled of beef stew and citrus floor polish. As she stepped into the foyer, the hardwood floors creaked under her feet.

"To be honest, your grandmother stopped taking care of the place after her first heart attack," Isla admitted sadly. "She let me take over things, but it was hard to get her to approve any of the proposed renovations. A few months before she died, there was a flood in the library and many books were badly damaged."

"I heard," Charlotte said with a nod. It was one of the reasons she had agreed to return.

"I can't wait to see what you do with the books," Isla said. "I follow you on Instagram, you know."

Charlotte smiled. She had started binding books a few years ago and had started a social media account to keep track of her progress. She hadn't expected to get more than just a few followers, but some of her posts had gotten some attention, and now she had a small but loyal following of about fifty people. But in truth, she was mostly looking forward to the challenges awaiting her in the library.

As they walked through the house, Charlotte spotted several projects that would need to be done. In some places, the wooden floors had been damaged, and there were some holes in the floor. Most of the rooms needed to be repainted, and she knew there were probably a million other things that she didn't even know about.

"Here we are," Isla said, opening the door to Charlotte's bedroom.

When Charlotte had visited the manor as a child, she had always stayed in a room that overlooked the country road leading up to the house. It was a large room with a four-poster bed and a window nook. She considered bringing a desk up to the room so that she could work there, but then she remembered that there was a whole office downstairs.

She couldn't believe that she would share the same working space as her grandfather, who had been an investment broker. Her copyediting work seemed trivial by comparison. Charlotte's grandfather had passed away when she was around ten years old, and she remembered that her grandmother never quite got over the loss of her husband. They were undoubtedly soulmates, and Charlotte couldn't comprehend such a loss.

"Dinner will be done around six," Isla said, standing awkwardly by the door.

Charlotte frowned. She couldn't remember Isla ever being awkward around her.

"I forgot you do all the cooking," Charlotte said. "How much do you do around here?"

"I spent most of my time taking care of your grandmother for the past few years," Isla said with a shrug. She looked like she wanted to say more, but she closed her mouth and averted her gaze. "I hope you settle in quickly."

With that, she walked out of the room with her head bowed.

"That was weird," Charlotte muttered as Archimedes jumped onto the bed.

He gave her a long look before curling up on one of the pillows and falling asleep. Meanwhile, Roma sat by the window, staring at the garden below. Charlotte walked over to the window and looked out at the garden. When she was a child, the gardens had always been well maintained, but now they were a tangled mass of overgrown weeds and bushes.

As she stared down at the plants, she started feeling overwhelmed. There was so much to do and so much to get used to. Charlotte barely knew anyone in town anymore, and she would have to get used to a whole new way of life.

She took a few deep calming breaths like her therapist had taught her and decided to go for a walk. Apparently, fresh air was always good at easing anxiety.

"Come on, Roma," she said, scooping the cat in her arms, "let's go for a walk."

They walked down the stairs and hurried outside. Charlotte could hear Isla walking around in the kitchen, talking to someone on the phone. When she heard Isla's voice, she walked toward the kitchen.

She wasn't sure what she was going to say, but she felt that she had to do something to ease the awkwardness between them. As she walked, she overheard snippets of Isla's conversation.

"No, I haven't told her yet." Isla sighed. "There hasn't been any time. She just got here. Honestly...I don't know what I'm going to do."

Charlotte's heart stopped in her chest when she heard that Isla was talking about her. She was about to reveal herself, but thought the better of it and stayed where she was. Unfortunately, the conversation quickly changed.

"You're right," Isla said, "I'll give it some time. She doesn't need to know yet. Hmm? Oh yeah, we have some apples outside; you're welcome to have some."

Charlotte chose not to go into the kitchen and continued outside. As soon as they were out of the house, Roma wriggled in Charlotte's arms, and Charlotte let her go. The cat was delighted by the garden and immediately jumped into the long grass.

"No, don't go too far…" Charlotte tried.

She probably shouldn't have let Roma go, but she was distracted by what she had heard in the kitchen. What was Isla worried about telling her?

Charlotte tried to keep track of Roma, but soon she couldn't see the cat anymore. She sighed and started walking down the cracked garden path. Eventually, the path became so overgrown and she heard rustling coming from a bush to her left. Roma had somehow made her way close to the stone fence. As Charlotte stepped, she felt the ground sag slightly beneath her feet.

Weird.

As she was about to step away, she heard Isla's voice coming from the front door.

"Careful, Charlotte!" Isla called. "There's an old well somewhere there…"

The ground gave way beneath Charlotte's feet, and she felt herself drop into a deep, dark hole. When she hit the bottom, she landed painfully on her feet, and her ankle gave way so that she hit her head on the side of the wall.

"Are you okay?" Isla shouted, her head appearing over the side of the hole a few seconds later.

The bottom of the well was mostly dry, but the ground was squishy and damp. Charlotte rubbed her forehead and grimaced. Thankfully, the well hadn't been too deep, and except for her head and ankle, she seemed fine.

"I'm okay," Charlotte said, "but I don't know how I'm going to get out."

"Don't worry," Isla said, "we have a ladder in the shed. I'll go get it."

Charlotte nodded and took her phone out of her pocket. She switched on the "torch" and looked around. The well's walls had been made out of river stones that still stuck out of the wall. While she waited for Isla, she sat down and checked her ankle. There wasn't much space, as the well was only wide enough for her to put one arm out. As she sat down, she felt something hard and smooth underneath her.

She assumed it was a rock, but when she shone the torch on it, she saw that it was almost perfectly rounded, and it was a strange ivory color. Her hands shook as she brushed some of the mud away and revealed the skull's eye sockets.

CHAPTER TWO

*A*s soon as Charlotte had gotten out of the well, she had called the police.

"I can't believe this is happening," she told Isla as they watched the police climb into the well.

The police had set up several powerful lights and had put plastic around the well. Roma was playing with the edge of the plastic, and every now and then a policeman tried to shoo her away, but she'd always make her way right back.

"This isn't how I imagined your first night back home going," Isla said with a grimace.

"Has anyone gone missing around here lately?" Charlotte asked, staring at the hole.

She still hadn't gotten over the feeling of shock that assaulted her when she'd realized that she was staring at a human skull. Charlotte had never even seen a dead person before, so she'd felt shaken to her core.

"Not that I can think of," Isla said, "and we would have known if someone went missing. This is a small community."

"Hey, Charlotte," one of the detectives said, walking up to her, "I didn't hear you were back in town. Hi, Isla."

Isla smiled and waved at him.

"Hi, Brandon," Charlotte said, crossing her arms over her chest. "Yeah, I told Nat that I was coming back."

Brandon nodded knowingly. Natalie Scott was one of Charlotte's closest friends. She also happened to be Brandon's ex-wife. It had been a messy divorce, and Charlotte had stayed firmly on Nat's side throughout the process.

"Right," Brandon said with a slight grimace. "Sorry about this mess. We'll get the body moved. As soon as Nat tells us who this is, we can let you know how long your garden will be a crime scene."

Nat also happened to be the county coroner.

"Sure," Charlotte said, and Brandon nodded at her before he walked off.

"That well has been covered up ever since I first started working here," Isla said thoughtfully. "I wasn't even completely sure where it was until you fell through it."

"Yeah, the wood felt old when it gave way," Charlotte said. "I guess the body must be old."

"Probably. I guess we'll have to wait and see."

Charlotte sent Nat a quick text message, warning her that a body was incoming. She also asked Nat to provide her with an update as soon as Nat figured out who it was. Nat replied with a thumbs-up emoji.

The next few days, Charlotte spent her time catching up with work and trying to get used to the massive, drafty manor. She was so busy that she didn't have any time to get to the library. She checked on it once or twice, and thankfully, most of the books were still intact.

One morning, while she was sorting through the books, she got a message from Nat. She had identified the body. Roma was playing nearby while Archimedes was asleep on Charlotte's office chair.

Charlotte felt a thrill go through her. She quickly got ready to leave, and decided to leave the cats at home. As she left the house, she saw that her neighbor's gate was open. She hadn't met the neighbor yet, but his garden was much neater than hers, with the exception of a supremely ugly gnome which stood on the neighbor's fence.

Charlotte shuddered; there was no accounting for taste. As soon as the gnome was out of sight, she forgot it as she raced down to the medical examiner's building. It was a drab building at the end of town located next to the old stone police station. She kept a careful eye out for Brandon. The last thing she wanted was an awkward run-in.

She walked over to Nat's office and let herself in.

"Hey," Nat said with a wide smile.

Nat was almost as tall as Charlotte, with thick chestnut-colored hair and deep-blue eyes, while Charlotte had lighter brown hair and light-green eyes. Nat's hair was done up in a bun, and she wore a white lab coat with several pens occupying the front pocket. Nat was incredibly clever, but she always looked frazzled, which was likely due to her lack of organizational skills.

"I can't believe it's taken me this long to get over to you," Charlotte said with a grimace. "I'm sorry; things have been crazy."

"Don't worry," Nat said, waving her hand dismissively. "I could have taken the initiative too. It's just that things have been difficult with work and Amy lately…"

Amy was Nat and Brandon's thirteen-year-old daughter. She was a sweet girl who loved reading and science. Unfortunately, the divorce had been tough on her, and she was becoming increasingly rebellious. The last time Nat and Charlotte had spoken, Nat had admitted that they were going to family therapy in order to help Amy.

"I completely understand," Charlotte said. "I mean, I only have to look after Roma and Archimedes, and some days that's almost too much to handle."

Nat smiled, and they spent a few minutes catching up. While it was nice chatting with Nat, Charlotte couldn't keep her curiosity from spilling over.

"We'll need to get dinner sometime so that we can catch up properly," Charlotte said, tapping her foot nervously. "I asked you to let me know about the body because I can't shake the feeling that I need to do something, you know?"

"I can imagine it must have been traumatic for you, falling in the well like that," Nat said sympathetically. "I'm just happy that I'm able to help. It appears that this body is about a hundred years old. The victim is female and was likely in her early twenties."

"Victim?" Charlotte echoed.

"I don't know how many young girls end up in boarded-up wells, do you?" Nat asked good-naturedly.

Nat was extremely clever, and she could come off as condescending to people who weren't used to her. Charlotte knew better—Nat was one of the nicest people on earth.

"Fair enough," Charlotte said. "Do the police know who it might be?"

"Yeah, given the age of the remains and the description of the victim, they think that this is likely Ivy Stanhope."

Charlotte frowned. She knew the Stanhope name. Everyone in Green Oaks did, since the mine used to employ thousands of townsfolk at one point. The original mine had closed, but there were still other Stanhope mines in the country. But Charlotte had never heard of Ivy Stanhope before.

"I forgot you're not a local," Nat said with a grimace. "So, Ivy was a local socialite who went missing in the 1920s. It was a massive scandal back then. Apparently, she had been dating one of the servants, Martin something or other, in secret, so everyone thought that they either ran off together or he got rid of her."

"Well, I guess we know what happened now," Charlotte said, "although the police will have their work cut out for them figuring out if the boyfriend actually did it."

"Oh, the police aren't going to do anything about it."

"What?" Charlotte asked in shock. "Why not?"

"The local cops work a large part of the county, and some of the surrounding towns don't even have police stations so they're stretched thin. They don't have the time or inclination to solve a hundred-year-old murder."

Charlotte burned with indignation. "That girl deserves justice. I mean, someone stuffed her into a well and closed it up over her. That's so messed up. Her parents died thinking that she ran away."

Nat sighed. "I agree that it's a tragedy, but life moves on. If the police aren't going to do something about it, then I can't argue. I sent some bone samples to the labs, and we're going to test to see if it really is Ivy Stanhope. My money is on it being her, and then we'll let her closest living relative know."

"Do we know who that is?"

"Kenan Stanhope. I think he'd be Ivy's second or third cousin twice removed or something. Look, I have no idea how the Stanhope family tree works; you're going to have to ask the local historian, Annette Pass. She's obsessed with this kind of thing. Kenan and Annette are working on opening a local museum. I don't see the point, but what does my opinion matter?"

Charlotte blanched at the thought of tracking down a strange woman just to ask her questions about one of the town's most influential families. No, it would be too weird. The mere thought of it made her chest tight, and she shook her head.

"I'm sorry," Nat said with a grimace, "I think it's best

if we just let this one go. It's a real shame what happened to Ivy, but the poor girl's been dead for over a hundred years. It's not like anyone's waiting for her to come home anymore."

"I guess, but it just feels wrong." Charlotte sighed. "When I found her body, it felt like this monumental event. I kind of expected something to come from it, you know? Finding a body shouldn't end like this. It's supposed to lead to an investigation, and we're supposed to get answers."

"Life is unfair," Nat said, shaking her head sadly. "Kenan will probably want to do something for her. Maybe he'll bury her with her family. That's a nice ending, I suppose."

Charlotte nodded, but she didn't quite agree. Although she knew next to nothing about Ivy, she still felt that the young woman deserved more than a hundred years at the bottom of a well then a quiet, muted burial.

The two women spent a few more minutes talking before Nat had to get back to work. As Charlotte got into her car, she felt a crushing feeling of disappointment. A wild thought occurred to her. What if she tried to find out what had happened to Ivy?

It seemed wildly impossible, but so did moving across the country to live in an old manor. Maybe Charlotte wasn't done surprising herself yet. She considered the possibility all the way home, and as she pulled into her driveway, she spotted something strange.

To her horror, the extremely ugly gnome was sitting on top of the fence, staring at her. She put the car in park and got out, stepping closer to the fence. The gnome was made out of ceramic and had an ugly green little coat. The worst part was its horribly engorged eyes and grimace. As she held the gnome in her hand, she shuddered.

The hairs on the back of her neck stood up, and she got the eerie feeling that she was being watched. Charlotte looked around suspiciously before walking over to her neighbor's property and propping the gnome on their fence. Unfortunately, she couldn't shake the feeling that someone had been watching her as she got back in her car and drove toward the house.

CHAPTER THREE

*C*harlotte tried to carry on with her routine, she really did. However, she kept thinking about the young woman that she'd found at the bottom of the well. One morning, she was sitting in the garden, staring at the top of the well while Roma hopped among the weeds.

"I had a feeling I'd find you out here," Isla said, walking up behind her.

Charlotte smiled wanly at Isla and looked over at Roma. The cat was staring at something moving in the long grass, her pupils narrowed into thin slits.

It was a cold day, as it had rained the previous night. The grass was still damp, but Charlotte didn't mind. Overhead, the sky was overcast, and a chill lingered in the air. She was dressed in a cable-knit sweater and an old pair of jeans.

"I know they covered it up, but I still get the heebie-jeebies when I look over there," Isla said as she sat down next to Charlotte and crossed her legs.

The day after Charlotte had gone to talk to Nat, two policemen came over and took down the police tape. It was no longer an active crime scene, so Isla had called a handyman who closed the top of the well with sturdy wooden beams.

"You've been quiet," Isla said, tilting her head as she looked at Charlotte. "Are you avoiding me?"

Isla made a pretty picture in her light-blue sweater with her blonde hair hanging around her shoulders. When she tilted her head, all her hair fell to one side and reminded Charlotte of a waterfall. Charlotte envied how Isla could be so direct when she struggled to find any words at all.

"No," Charlotte lied, her cheeks turning red as she stared at the well.

She was still thinking about that mysterious phone call that she had overheard. What was Isla afraid to tell her? In all honesty, Charlotte couldn't handle any more bad news, and the last thing she needed was for Isla to tell her that she was leaving. There was no way Charlotte would be able to handle everything that needed to be done in the house by herself.

"C'mon," Isla urged, bumping Charlotte's shoulder with her own, "I've known you long enough to know when something's bothering you."

Charlotte frowned. "It feels wrong...all of this! I found a girl down there; the world should be...different. It's like this terrible thing happened, and the world doesn't even have the decency to stop for a second. It's as if her life never even mattered."

She stopped talking and bit her lip. Her words had surprised herself, but she still had more to say. It was something that had been bothering her before she fell through the well and had nothing to do with Ivy Stanhope at all.

"She meant a whole lot to some people," Charlotte said softly. "How is it that I'm the only one who seems to be bothered by this?"

Isla listened patiently while Charlotte ranted then put a comforting hand on Charlotte's arm. Meanwhile, Roma pounced suddenly on something. When she looked up, she had a cricket in her mouth. The cricket tried to jump away, and its flailing legs tickled Roma's nose. Roma scrunched up her nose and dropped the cricket in disgust.

"You're not the only one who's hurting," Isla said

softly. "We all miss her, you know. Your grandmother was a force for good in this town."

Charlotte hugged her knees to her chest and didn't say anything.

"Sometimes, we need to do something more than simply feel our grief," Isla said. "Sometimes we need to take action."

"What can I do about my grandmother dying? It's the most natural thing in the world, isn't it? Grandchildren lose their grandparents all the time. It's the most common form of grief."

"That's the cynic in you speaking," Isla said. "I was wrecked for years after my grandmother died, and we weren't even as close as you and Jenny."

Charlotte grimaced. She hadn't been there when her grandmother died. In fact, they hadn't seen each other in person in over three years. It was something that haunted her.

"Some people start charities, others take on projects to commemorate their loved ones," Isla continued, "but you know what I think? You should do something for Ivy. No one else is going to do it."

Are you crazy? The words were at the tip of Charlotte's tongue, but she didn't say them out loud.

"Think about it," Isla said, "you could do some research and find out more about her. That would make her more than just a girl at the bottom of a well to you. I think you're bothered because you think you're expected to just pick up and move on. You don't have to do that."

It makes sense, in a weird kind of way. Charlotte chewed on her bottom lip.

"I wouldn't know where to begin," Charlotte admitted.

"Start at the historical society," Isla suggested. "The town historian, Annette something, convinced the old Methodist church to donate their original church building to the society so that they could preserve some of the town's history there. She's over there most days digging through old documents and stuff. She loves talking about history, and I'm sure she'd be thrilled to have someone new to lecture."

"I don't know…" Charlotte said with a wince. "I'm not exactly the type of person who goes up to strangers and asks them for a favor. She might be busy…"

"Ivy had her whole life ahead of her," Isla reminded her. "She should be more than just the girl in the well, don't you think?"

She's right. Charlotte nodded.

"Besides, you can't spend all your time moping in the garden," Isla said. "You need to do something to move on."

"I guess," Charlotte said with a wry smile.

"There ya go," Isla said proudly.

Charlotte felt herself sit up straighter. Isla's pride in her gave her some confidence that she would succeed.

"Will you come with?" Charlotte asked nervously.

"I would have loved to," Isla said with a wince, "but I need to wait for the handyman—you know Beau. He said he'd be around to fix the gutters today."

She just wants to be alone when Beau gets here. The thought caused Charlotte to smile mischievously.

"I don't know why you're smiling like that," Isla said, raising an eyebrow.

"Sure, you don't," Charlotte said teasingly as she got up.

As she walked, she picked Roma up and headed to the car. She knew she had to get going before all her courage left her. Archimedes was sleeping nearby on a windowsill. His orange fur gleamed in the sun, and he looked blissful. She knew if she took him with, he would only yell at her the entire time.

"Sleep well, baby cat," Charlotte said, stroking his head before she got into the car.

Roma, on the other hand, was excited to be going out on an adventure. As the car started moving, she stood on her hind legs and put her front legs on the side of the car so that she could look out the window.

"We're going on an adventure, Roma," Charlotte said, trying to psych herself up for what lay ahead.

When she got to the old church, she stopped the car and took a few deep breaths. Roma turned back and meowed inquisitively, which gave Charlotte the courage she needed to get out of the car. The old church was made out of stone that had been cut out of a nearby mountain. There were still scrape marks on the stone where the original workers had cut the stone into blocks.

It was a simple building with an arched doorway and a bell tower at the top. Charlotte knocked on the heavy wooden door, but as her knuckles touched the wood, the door swung open, and she tentatively stepped in.

Roma darted in ahead of her, and Charlotte quickly hurried in to catch her. The inside of the church was warm thanks to the fire that was roaring in the fireplace.

"Hello?" Charlotte called.

There were several displays that had been set up and a desk filled with papers. The room was completely empty. Charlotte sighed. The light streamed in through the stained-glass windows depicting Christ's resurrection.

As she was about to leave, a diminutive woman with a sharp, hooked nose and glasses walked into the room with her head buried in a document.

"Hi?" Charlotte said, her voice soft.

The woman looked up in surprise, revealing her round, cherubic face. "Oh, hi...sorry, the museum isn't open yet."

"Oh, okay..." Charlotte said. "Uh, actually, I'm not here for that. I wanted to talk to the town historian, Annette."

"Is that what they're calling me?" the woman asked in amusement, putting the document on a nearby display.

"You must be Annette," Charlotte said, her cheeks warming up. "I'm Charlotte, I moved into—"

"You're Jenny's granddaughter," Annette said with a knowing look.

Annette didn't look much older than Charlotte, but Charlotte didn't feel like the woman was one of her peers. For one thing, Annette looked like a college professor, and Charlotte looked like a student.

"That's right," Charlotte said, "I wanted to ask you about—"

"You're the one who found Ivy Stanhope," Annette said, her eyes brightening. "I'll bet you're here to find out what happened to her. Aren't you?"

Charlotte didn't know what to say because it seemed like Annette would only interrupt her if she did. She nodded.

"Awesome," Annette breathed, revealing her age. "Okay, so check this out."

She waved Charlotte over. Charlotte looked over at Roma, who was busy investigating the room. When Charlotte got closer, she saw the display that Annette was standing in front of was exclusively about Ivy.

The display case was filled with Ivy's comb, her compact mirror, a pair of gloves and a few of her letters. A mannequin was dressed in Ivy's clothes and a portrait of Ivy hung over the wall. It was creepy. Charlotte shivered. The display looked like a shrine to the missing girl.

"Ivy Stanhope was the sole heiress to the Stanhope fortune," Annette explained excitedly. "She was a fashionable socialite and had a bright future. She and her cousin, Kingsley, all but ran this town after her father died of Spanish Influenza."

"Interesting," Charlotte said lamely when Annette turned to her expectantly.

Charlotte noticed that Annette's eyes were a charming mix of green and brown that created a unique hazel mixture.

"You have no idea," Annette said enthusiastically. "Ivy was distinguished and well-mannered; she was set to marry Elias Rivera, of the Rivera Oil Company. Their betrothal made front-page news in Boston."

"Was it a slow news day?" Charlotte asked in amusement.

Annette gave her an unimpressed look, and Charlotte grimaced.

"About two days before her wedding, Ivy went missing," Annette said in a breathless tone. "There were rumors that Ivy had run off with Martin Baker, a local boy. Apparently, they had been seeing each other during the war years, and Martin had only just returned. We now know that she never went anywhere."

"What happened to Martin?"

"He also went missing," Annette said with a shrug. "His family was convinced that something bad had happened to him too, but there's no body, so we have to assume that he killed Ivy."

"I mean, it makes sense," Charlotte said thoughtfully. "If they were dating during the war then he came back to find her engaged to someone else…"

"That's the current theory," Annette said, waving her hand dismissively. She stared up at Ivy's portrait with an intense expression. "I think something else happened."

"What?" Charlotte asked curiously.

"You found her in the well, right?" Annette asked, and Charlotte nodded quickly. "Yeah, so guess who rented that house between the years of 1920 and 1922?"

Charlotte shrugged.

"None other than Elias Rivera. Maybe Ivy changed her mind about marrying him when her old flame turned up in town. I'm thinking a guy like Elias wasn't used to rejection and didn't take her leaving too kindly. One way or another, I'm going to find out. Elias's great-grandson lives in town. His name is Jacob Haskins. He's been dodging me, but when I get hold of him, I'm going to make sure he tells me everything he knows about Elias. Mark my words, Elias Rivera had something to do with Ivy's murder."

CHAPTER FOUR

nnette stated her theory as if it was a confirmed fact. Charlotte admired how Annette approached the world with such confidence. Her theory sounded plausible. It occurred to Charlotte that Ivy lived a whole life filled with people who were no longer around. And yet, everyone still had their own opinions about what had happened. Was there any way to know what had really happened to Ivy?

"That's a good point," Charlotte said to Annette. "What day did she go missing?"

"The twelfth of December, 1922," Annette said. "Elias Rivera hosted a party the night before, and Kingsley was the one who reported her missing. He was frantic."

Kingsley Stanhope's name kept popping up. She didn't know anyone who was as close to their cousin as

Kingsley and Ivy seemed to be. Was there more to the story? After all, he was the one who had inherited everything after Ivy went missing.

"Oh, and there's one more thing," Annette said, her eyes brightening. "Here." She stepped up to the display and opened a drawer at the bottom. She pulled a latex glove onto her hand and dug through a clear plastic file until she found a letter.

The paper was yellowed with age, and the ink was faded to gray instead of black. The letters were curly and slanted.

"This letter is from a maid in the Stanhope household," Annette said triumphantly. "The maid, Betsy, worked at the party that night and left sometime after everyone left. Read it."

Charlotte took the letter and squinted at the page. The words were nearly illegible. Roma jumped into a nearby box, and Charlotte looked up to make sure the cat wasn't causing too much trouble. Roma poked her head over the top of the box, her pupils dilated. Her tail flicked behind her.

"Oh, let me read that for you," Annette said, ripping the letter out of her hands impatiently. "'Dear Mama, I was disappointed that I wasn't able to see you this Sunday past. Master Stanhope loaned us to Master Rivera for the evening to serve at his dinner party.

There were many in attendance, and the guests danced to their heart's content. You may have heard by now that Mistress Stanhope has gone missing. I thought this would touch you personally as you served her mama, Eleanor. Mistress Stanhope seemed to be in good spirits for most of the evening, but she and Master Rivera spent most of the evening carefully avoiding each other. The other maids gossiped and stated that her reticence was on account of Martin Baker's sudden return to Green Oaks.'"

Charlotte frowned. She didn't see how the letter proved Annette's theory. It was only natural that Ivy would avoid her fiancé if her ex was in town. Maybe she'd had a lot on her mind.

"'Mistress Stanhope remained at the manor during the entirety of the party,'" Annette continued reading. "'She and Master Rivera were deep in conversation before she left. He was in a mood most foul when she left. One of the maids heard him breaking something in his office before he left in the night after her. I'm sure that her disappearance will spell disaster for young Martin. It is a shame, since he seemed to be a nice boy when I last spoke to him. I am in half a mind to tell the sheriff what I saw, but the other girls told me to keep it to myself. No one wants to run afoul of Master Rivera. Perhaps I should approach

Master Kingsley who seems beside himself with fear. Don't tell anyone about this, Mama, but I heard him pacing in his room last night. It sounded as though he was crying. It's only natural given how close they were.'"

Charlotte's eyebrows flew upward, and she covered her mouth with her hand.

"That's what I thought," Annette said. "The librarian found this letter in an old Bible in a box of donated books back in the seventies. Of course, no one thought much about it back then. I think it shines light on the whole situation now."

"Wow," Charlotte said, "I can only imagine what happened when Elias caught up with her."

"I'll tell you what happened," Annette said darkly. "Look at how small Ivy was."

She gestured at a picture in an old newspaper on display. Charlotte stepped forward and studied the picture. Ivy was standing between two tall men. Elias was on her right, and Kingsley was on her left. Ivy's dark hair was cut into a bob, and her lips were painted with dark lipstick. She looked impossibly glamorous in her flapper's outfit. Her arms held Elias and Kingsley close, as if she owned them both.

Elias was looking down at her with an enraptured expression. He was handsome with an angular jaw and thick eyebrows. Kingsley was fairer, and he was looking at something or someone off-camera.

"You know who you should talk to?" Annette said. "Kenan Stanhope still lives in town. He's Kingsley's great-grandson or something. He even lives in the old Stanhope mansion."

"I don't know..." Charlotte said, uncomfortable with the thought of bothering one of Ivy's distant relatives.

"Go," Annette said firmly. "He won't talk to me, but if you tell him that you're looking into Ivy's death—"

"I'm not, though," Charlotte said quickly, interrupting Annette for once. "I mean, I'm not looking into her death. I was just curious, that's all."

"I see," Annette said, pursing her lips. "That's a real shame. If it were me, I'd want to know what happened to poor Ivy. I mean, your grandmother lived her whole life in that house, and she never even knew about Ivy being in the well."

Charlotte bristled. She wanted to tell Annette that it was none of her business, and it certainly wasn't her grandmother's fault that there had been a body in the well the whole time. Instead, she smiled weakly and looked away.

"Well, I'm sure I'll see you at the museum's grand opening," Annette said, before walking away.

Charlotte sighed and looked up at the portrait of Ivy.

The young woman seemed to be smiling at a secret joke as she stared right at Charlotte, and Charlotte felt an immense guilt filling her.

"I'm sorry," Charlotte told Ivy before she picked Roma up and walked away.

The guilt didn't go away, and when Charlotte pulled up to the house, she felt more awful than when she'd left. As she got out of her car, she spotted Beau working on the gutters. He was ruggedly handsome with sandy-blond hair and a strong frame. Isla stood at the bottom of his ladder, chatting easily with him.

When Isla saw Charlotte, she frowned and hurried over.

"What's wrong?" Isla asked in concern.

Charlotte told her everything, and Isla frowned. "That Annette certainly is a troublemaker. She had no business making you feel guilty over something you can't control."

Charlotte sighed. "I know, but I still feel bad about it. I mean, the least I could do is go talk to Kenan, but the thought of talking to him makes me so nervous."

"Aw, honey," Isla said sympathetically, "would it help if I came with you?"

Charlotte nodded then quickly shook her head. "No, you're here with Beau…"

"Don't you worry about it," Isla said, shaking her

head quickly, her cheeks turning pink. "Beau is going to carry on here. Let's go talk to Kenan."

"Thanks, Isla," Charlotte said gratefully. "I don't know what I would do without you."

Isla smiled weakly and looked away. It looked to Charlotte that Isla felt guilty about something, and Charlotte felt a twinge of anxiety.

They got into the car, and Roma climbed happily onto Isla's lap. Isla directed her to the Stanhope Estate which was about twenty minutes out of town. It was much larger than Charlotte's house and even had a small guardhouse by the gate.

"Do you have an appointment?" the security guard asked with a blank expression as he stood by Charlotte's window.

"No, but tell Kenan he needs to talk to us," Isla said, leaning over Charlotte so that she could talk to the security guard. "It's about Ivy, and he can either choose to talk to us now or to Annette later."

"Right," the security guard said, looking bored. "I'll see what I can do."

Isla smiled knowingly at Charlotte, and a minute later, the large gate opened automatically. The security guard motioned for them to go through, and Charlotte drove onto the estate. She hadn't expected them to get that far.

Charlotte drove up the lane toward the house. It was a beautiful drive as someone had planted trees all along the driveway so that the branches met over the lane in a beautiful arch. The house was even more beautiful with a white façade and large pillars that supported the entrance.

She saw Kenan standing out front and recognized him because he was the spitting image of Kingsley Stanhope. He had the same light-blond hair and strong features.

"Hey there," he said with a friendly smile as they got out of the car.

It looked like Kenan was in his early forties with crow's feet around his eyes. His smile was disarming, and Charlotte found herself looking at Isla to take the lead.

"Hello," Isla said, "I haven't seen you in forever. How have you been?"

"Oh yes, I think we last saw each other at the fundraiser for the historical society," Kenan said with a chuckle. "That was an interesting evening. Annette was determined to make me feel like a complete embarrassment to the town for not donating my family's belongings."

Charlotte let out a knowing chuckle, which drew Kenan's gaze to her.

"I don't think I've had the pleasure of meeting you yet," Kenan said. "You must be Jenny's granddaughter."

"Charlotte," she said shyly, holding her hand out for him to shake.

"Nice to meet you, Charlotte. I hear you're the one who found Ivy. Thanks for that, by the way. It's something that's bothered me for years. My great-grandfather, Kingsley, was broken about it. You know, he was still talking about her when he died. He told me the whole story when I was about six years old. It's haunted me ever since."

"I'm so sorry," Charlotte said sincerely. "It's terrible that things ended this way."

She found that it was easy to talk to Kenan.

"I always thought she was dead," Kenan admitted, "and deep down, so did my great-grandfather. You see, there's no way she would have left him otherwise."

"I take it they were close," Isla said.

Roma had wandered out of the car and was sitting by Charlotte's feet, staring intently at Kenan's shoelaces.

"They grew up like siblings," Kenan said. "Kingsley's parent's died when he was a child, and so Ivy's family took him in. You'll see them together in nearly every photograph. Kingsley was only twenty-five when she went missing."

"Do you know who might have killed her?" Charlotte asked.

"Annette would have you think that it was old Elias Rivera," Kenan snorted, "but Kingsley always thought that it was Martin Baker's fault. You know... I think you should be able to make up your own mind. I have some of Ivy's old things in a trunk upstairs; would you like to look through it?"

Charlotte's heart swelled with hope, but she forced herself to nod calmly. The last thing she wanted was for Kenan to think she was crazy or something.

"Are you sure?" she asked carefully.

"You found her," Kenan pointed out. "I'm sure it's bothering you. Besides, I've had a lifetime to look through those things. Trust me, I know everything that's in there. I'd rather have you look through it than Annette. She'd only twist things to make Elias out to be the bad guy."

"I don't know if I'll find anything," Charlotte said, picking nervously at her thumbnail.

"I don't expect you to find anything new," Kenan said kindly, "but I trust you'll come to the same conclusion as I did about Martin Baker. There are some things that Kingsley chose to keep private to preserve her dignity. I think it's about time the world knows the truth about Ivy though."

CHAPTER FIVE

"Kenan seems like a nice guy," Charlotte said as they drove home.

Ivy's old suitcase was in the trunk, and she couldn't wait to get home to search through it. She tapped her fingers on the steering wheel as they waited at a red light.

"He is," Isla said, "and he's single too…"

Charlotte didn't say anything. She assumed that Isla was infatuated with Beau. Maybe she wanted to be with Kenan instead?

"He's not that much older than you," Isla continued, stroking Roma's head.

Roma was on Isla's lap. The cat purred so loudly that Charlotte could hear it over the radio.

"Wait," Charlotte said with a frown, "why would I

care how old he is?"

"I don't know," Isla said with a shrug, "I thought you two got along. Maybe if you're interested, you could see what happens. He's divorced, you know."

"No."

"Charlotte, you have to give the guy a chance before you say no," Isla said in amusement.

"No way. It's too awkward to even think about. No."

Charlotte was in no place to think about that sort of thing. Besides, Kenan was just being nice. If she read too much into his behavior, she ran the risk of being disappointed.

"I've never met someone so opposed to being in a relationship as you," Isla complained. "How are you ever going to settle down if you don't open yourself up to the possibility of love?"

"Maybe I don't want to settle down."

As they pulled into the driveway, Charlotte spotted a familiar ugly gnome. A wave of indignation rose up inside of her.

"You've got to be kidding me!" she said in frustration as she stopped the car outside of the gate.

"What?" Isla asked in confusion as Charlotte jumped out of the car. "What are you doing?"

Charlotte didn't say anything as she marched over, picked up the gnome, and put it firmly on her neighbor's lawn. She pushed it into the soft ground so that its bulbous brown shoes were firmly planted into the soil.

"Stay!" Charlotte commanded, glaring down at the thing.

"Oh, that's the neighbor's gnome," Isla said, tilting her head slightly. "I hate that thing. Remember Old Mrs. Bennett? She sold that house a few months ago. I never met the new owners, but I think it's an old couple."

"If they don't want the ugly gnome, then they should get rid of it instead of trying to pawn it off on me," Charlotte said in annoyance as she drove toward the house.

"Why don't you just throw it away if you hate it so much?" Isla asked in confusion. Her eyes brightened when she saw Beau still working on the gutters.

"It's the principle of the matter," Charlotte said firmly. "Besides, I don't want to throw it away. It feels wrong. It's been there since I first started coming around here as a kid. My grandmother used to say it kept all the other ugly things out of the neighborhood. You know, like crime and stuff."

"That makes no sense," Isla said with a chuckle.

"You know my grandmother," Charlotte said, shrugging her shoulders. "Come on, Roma. Let's go."

Charlotte walked to the back of the car and took the suitcase out of the trunk. It was a solid leather suitcase with Ivy's initials embossed on the front in gold lettering.

"Do you need help with that?" Isla asked.

Isla's eyes kept drifting over to Beau, and Charlotte saw that he was trying very hard not to keep looking over at them. She smiled to herself.

"No, I'll be okay," Charlotte said before she took the suitcase inside.

Roma chose to stay outside, and when Charlotte walked inside, she went over to the living room. Archimedes was still lying on the windowsill, enjoying the sun. She sat close to him and opened the suitcase.

There were a few dresses inside, two pairs of shoes, and an old copy of *Pride and Prejudice* with Ivy's child-like handwriting in the front. Charlotte smiled to herself and flipped through the book. Ivy had made several annotations in the margins, and Charlotte enjoyed going through it to see what Ivy had thought of the story.

"I think Annette would kill to get her hands on this," Charlotte told Archimedes.

The cat sat up slightly and began licking his paw. In between grooming himself, he would look over at Charlotte and blink slowly. She had read somewhere that if a cat blinked slowly at a person, it likely trusted them. Charlotte was overcome with the need to cuddle him, but gently scratched the spot behind his ear instead.

"Look, here she wrote, 'Way to go, Lizzie!' It's so sweet," Charlotte murmured, as she continued flipping through the book.

When she got to the end of the book, where Elizabeth and Darcy finally got together, she spotted one of Ivy's annotations.

Darcy's dreamy, but he can't compare to my Martin!

Charlotte smiled, feeling touched by the glimpse into Ivy and Martin's relationship. And then she remembered how their story ended. It seemed strange to her that they knew nothing about what had happened to Martin. While it seemed like everyone was forgetting about Ivy, it was even worse for Martin. Some people were painting him as a murderer, but no one could ask his side of the story since he had gone missing around the same time as Ivy.

"What happened to you?" Charlotte asked out loud.

She leaned back in her armchair and looked out the window. The sun was peeking through the clouds, and it seemed that Archimedes had found the only spot in the house where there was any sun.

"This can't be it," Charlotte said, as she looked down at the book.

She methodically took everything out of the suitcase, and that's when she happened on a bundle of letters. There were several letters bound with string, and all of them were from Ivy's friends and acquaintances. However, they were all dated after her disappearance.

Dear Kingsley,

I was so disturbed to hear of Ivy's disappearance. Please let us know if there is anything that we can do to help. If it is of any consequence, I would like you to know that I met with Ivy at Elias' soiree last night, and she seemed to be in high spirits. There was no indication that she would run off of her own accord.
Granted, you already knew that, but I thought some assurance would help silence any doubts. Chin up, old boy! We'll find her yet.

Sincerely,

Rowling

"That's weird," Charlotte said with a frown. "The maid said that Ivy seemed strange that night. Maybe this Rowling guy never paid much attention to Ivy?"

Archimedes responded by sneezing then promptly began licking himself again.

"You're probably the most unhelpful cat I've ever met," Charlotte said, poking Archimedes' fat stomach.

Archimedes immediately grabbed her finger in his paw and gave it a lick. She smiled at him and rubbed his head before looking at the rest of the letters. They all gave an insight into the people around Ivy.

Dearest Kingsley,

My darling Kingsley, we were terribly distraught when we learned of dear Ivy's disappearance. Mama says you simply must join us for dinner this week so that we might be able to take care of you.

I truly enjoyed our dance at Elias Rivera's party. Would you do me the honor of calling on me so that we might be able to discuss where Ivy might have run off to after the party? I asked her not to leave early, but you know how contrary our Ivy can be!

There's word in the town that a certain Mr. Baker has returned after all this time. I recall that you were concerned about his effect on Ivy's behavior. I simply adore our Ivy, but she certainly knew how to cause trouble. You mustn't blame her too much, darling Kingsley. That Martin Baker is a real troublemaker. And you know what they say about his temper! I firmly believe that Ivy is simply hiding from that brute and that she'll be back in due course. I know it's frustrating, but I am certain that you have the necessary patience. My mama says that you must be a saint.

Of course, we need to take pity on her, as she didn't have a lot of guidance while you were away. You mentioned that you were grateful that I was here to guide her. I'll always be here to assist you in any way that I can.

Lovingly,

Katherine

"Katherine sounds like a bad friend," Charlotte said, wrinkling her nose in disgust. "I wonder if poor Ivy had any real friends."

Charlotte sat there, surrounded by Ivy's things, and she felt a heavy sadness settle over her. All that was left of Ivy was a pile of old bones, a few articles of clothing, and a bundle of letters from people who pretended to care about her.

Charlotte sighed. "I hope Martin loved her well... unless he killed her..."

"Who are you talking to?" Isla asked as she walked into the room.

Charlotte turned bright red and shook her head. "No one. Well, just me. I was talking to myself. I know, it's weird."

"It's not that weird," Isla said, dropping onto a nearby chair. "Your grandmother used to have conversations with herself all the time. Sometimes, she'd ignore me so she could finish the conversation."

"I remember that," Charlotte said with a chuckle. "I always told her that people would think she was crazy, and she said that people would think she was crazier if she didn't talk to herself."

"That makes no sense," Isla said, shaking her head.

"I think it did." Charlotte shrugged. "It was a way for her to relieve stress and figure things out. If she stopped, she probably would have gone crazy for real. Then people would definitely think she was crazy, because it would be true, you know?"

"No," Isla said with a laugh, "but that's why she loved you so much. You were the only one who ever understood what she meant."

Charlotte liked that, but she didn't say anything. Instead, she read through the next letter. This time, her eyes widened when she read the letter.

Dear Ivy,

*As soon as I came home from the party, I wrote this
letter. Will you ever forgive me for leaving you like
that? I'm so terribly sorry. Please, please forgive me. I
know I was an awful friend, but I got so fed up with
waiting. You know how strict my father is! He all but
dragged me to the car at midnight. Why didn't you
come back from your meeting with Martin? Kingsley
was beside himself!*

*I can't help but think that something terrible has
happened to you. Perhaps in the morning, I will be
embarrassed that I sent this letter. Oh, I do hope that is
the case!*

*Please, please, please get home safely my dear Ivy. If
you're already home, please send word. I know you'll
be awfully vexed with me, but please send word that
you arrived safely. I promised I'd keep this from
Kingsley, and I will, but I truly think you shouldn't see
Martin anymore.*

*You keep extolling his virtues, but there was something
dark in his countenance this evening. I saw him
peeking through the window at Elias' house, I know*

you'll say I'm lying, but I'm not. You should have seen his face when he saw you dancing with Elias. Please, he's no good for you. I know he means you harm.

I'll be over first thing tomorrow morning. Please forgive me for leaving.

Love,

Elizabeth.

CHAPTER SIX

"*I* can't believe this," Isla said with a gasp as she examined the book in the light.

They were standing in the middle of the library in the manor.

When Charlotte had arrived, she had set up a work-table for herself which included all the tools she needed to rebind the covers of all the damaged books. Her grandmother had a lot of rare first edition books in the library, and Charlotte wanted to personalize each book cover. The first book she had chosen was a collection of Canterbury Tales. It was a thick book, and she had carefully removed the old, damaged cover.

In order to do it, she had used several sharp and precise tools to take the old cover off. Then she cut some cloth and glued it carefully to some sturdy cardboard and rebound the book. When the glue was dry, she used an embosser and carefully embossed some gold leaf into the borders. She also painted some scenes from the book on the inside.

Along with the golden border and embossed words, she had also etched the outline of several animal characters on the front. Charlotte had spent hours on it, but there were still a few things she wanted to tweak.

"This is so beautiful," Isla said, her eyes wide with wonder. "You've turned it into a real collector's piece!"

While Isla examined the book, Charlotte turned off the camera that she had trained on her workspace. Making videos of her work was a fun way to keep track of her progress, and she uploaded the videos to social media so that others could see what she was doing.

"You think?" Charlotte asked shyly. "I haven't painted the pages yet…"

"Oh, sweetie, this is gorgeous," Isla said firmly. "Your grandmother would have been so proud."

"Thanks," Charlotte said, scratching the back of her neck awkwardly.

While they were talking, Charlotte heard someone calling from the front door.

"Hello?" Annette called. "Is anyone here?"

Charlotte and Isla looked at each other in confusion.

"I wasn't expecting her," Charlotte said, "were you?"

"That's the thing about Annette," Isla said, rolling her eyes. "No one ever expects her. I'll see if I can get rid of her. Great job with the book; I think it's stunning."

When Isla was gone, Charlotte flipped the book open and thought about what kind of paint she should use on the edge of the pages. While she worked, Archimedes jumped up onto her table. She kept a careful eye on him, because the last time he had jumped onto her table, he had walked right through a tray of red paint. There were red paw prints all over the library floor, and Charlotte had no idea how she was going to clean it up.

If she used paint thinners, it would damage the hardwood floors, and no amount of scrubbing would get it off either. She was in a real bind.

"Stay away from the paint, ya hear?" Charlotte warned Archimedes.

He simply sniffed at her and turned his head away. The cat was so voluminous that he took up a fraction of the table. Charlotte had put him on a diet after his last vet visit, and he was extra moody as a result.

"There you are," Annette said, walking into the room with Isla trailing helplessly behind her. "Isla said you were too busy, but what I have to say is way too important."

"I highly doubt it," Isla grumbled.

Annette ignored her. "What did Kenan say? Did he give you the suitcase?"

Charlotte's eyes widened, and she looked over to Isla, who shrugged. They had no idea how Annette had gotten her information.

"Look, Annette," Charlotte said with a sigh, "I'm sorry, but I think you're wrong. Ivy was probably killed by Martin, and he left town. All of this happened over a hundred years ago now. Maybe we should leave it behind?"

She was lying, of course. Over the past few nights, she had lost a lot of sleep as she tried to figure out how to discover what had happened to Martin. She felt like an explorer in a new land. It was hard to know where to begin or how to find her way. Elizabeth's letter had been concerning and placed Ivy with Martin at some point in the evening, well after midnight. However, the maid, Betsy, had seen Ivy leave and stated that Elias followed her.

One way or another, it was extremely likely that Ivy's messy love life had gotten her killed.

"Are you kidding me?" Annette scoffed, crossing her arms over her chest. "Kenan got to you, didn't he? What was it, Charlotte? Was it his baby-blue eyes or his money?"

"I didn't know his eyes were baby blue," Isla said

smartly. "It's funny how you know exactly which shade of blue his eyes are, Annette."

"Whatever, Isla," Annette said, rolling her eyes. "I pay attention to my surroundings. You should try it some time."

"I'm sorry," Charlotte said, "I know you're invested in this, but I don't think I can help you anymore. I have too much on my plate right now."

"I have enough going on as it is," Annette said in annoyance. "Jacob Haskins threatened to file a restraining order against me, and now you're conspiring with Kenan."

"No one's conspiring with anyone," Charlotte said, trying to remain patient.

"And I can completely empathize with Jacob," Isla said in amusement, causing Annette to glare at her.

"Yeah, maybe leave him alone," Charlotte said. "He obviously doesn't have anything to share."

Charlotte got the feeling that Annette wasn't telling the full truth about what was going on with Jacob. There had to be a reason why he was thinking of filing a restraining order against her.

Annette's face turned red, and she stomped her foot angrily, as if she was a toddler.

"If I find out that you're holding out on me, you're

going to regret it," Annette said, wagging her finger at Charlotte before storming out.

"Why'd you lie to her?" Isla asked, leaning against the doorway.

"I lie when I'm nervous," Charlotte said, averting her gaze carefully. "I'm trying to stop."

A familiar feeling of shame enveloped her. She was always disappointed in herself when that happened. Charlotte tried to be honest, but it didn't always come easy.

"You don't look too broken up about it," Isla commented.

"Yeah, well, she made me mad when she barged in like that," Charlotte said, happy that Isla couldn't read her thoughts.

Isla shrugged. "Fair enough. So, did Nat get back to you about Martin's closest living relative?"

"Yeah, James Whittaker. He lives in a nursing home nearby. I'm supposed to see him at four during their visiting hours."

"Oh man," Isla said, shaking her head as she chuckled.

"What?"

"I was just imagining Annette's face when she finds out that you fooled her."

Charlotte tried to smile, but she still felt a niggling

pit of guilt in her stomach. She continued working on her book until it was time to leave.

James lived in a retirement village about two hours away. It was a pleasant place called Sunny Acres with several free-standing homes as well as a larger care facility where the older residents stayed once they needed more help.

"You've got to speak up when you talk to James," a nurse explained as she led Charlotte into the common room.

It was a large, airy space with a huge flat-screen TV, couches, and a cupboard full of board games in the corner. Although Charlotte struggled with new people, she always felt at ease with older folks. It was probably due to all the time she had spent with her grandmother as a child.

James was sitting alone in a corner in a wheelchair. He stared out the window thoughtfully.

"Hi, James."

Charlotte was careful to speak loud enough that he could hear her but not so loud that she was shouting at him.

James looked up at her. His eyes were a warm brown with a light film of age over them. His hair was completely white, and when he smiled, his lined face became softer.

"Hello there, girly," he said. "You told me you wanted to talk to me 'bout one of my relatives?"

"That's right. I wanted to find out if you knew anything about Martin Baker."

James nodded slowly and reached under his wheelchair. He produced a shoebox which he gave to her. "These are some old family photos. I thought you might appreciate them."

"Thank you," Charlotte said reverently.

He had given her something that he had held onto for most of his life. As she looked at the photos, she saw generations of the Whittaker and Baker families all intertwined.

"My grandmama was Martin's sister, you see," he explained. "She was there when it all went down. It ate her up real bad, and she always cried when she talked about him."

"I'm terribly sorry," Charlotte said, touching his hand gently.

"That's all right," James said with a shrug. "It ain't your fault. Besides, you're trying to find out the truth now, and that's something."

"Can you tell me anything about him?"

"Sure can," James said with a proud smile. "Martin was only seventeen when he signed up to join the war effort. Poor fella. He thought he was going to save the world all by himself then come right back and marry that sweet girl Ivy."

Charlotte leaned forward. Finally, she was finding out about the man who had supposedly murdered Ivy.

"My grandmama used to say that Martin was the kind of fool who was too pure for this world. You see, he was soft. Not in the head; more like he believed the best in the world even when that wasn't good for him. He and Ivy got together the summer before he left for the war. His big brother had gone and died. He figured that he oughta do something, else he'd be a coward."

"Poor Ivy," Charlotte murmured.

"Poor everyone." James sighed. "Anyhow, this fool goes off and fights 'em Germans, but the war messed him up real bad. He told Ivy that he wasn't the same man no more…well, he wrote to her. He told her to move on without him. My grandmama said the war took his head off and screwed it back the wrong way 'round."

"Do you think he was mentally ill?" Charlotte asked.

"Oh yeah, he had what we call PTSD, only they didn't have a word for it back then. They just thought that he was crazy or something."

"He didn't want her to be stuck with him," Charlotte realized.

"And she went off and got engaged to that Rivera

fella. My grandmama always said it was the biggest mistake that girl ever made. You see, when Ivy was engaged, Martin was released from that loony bin they stuck him in after the war. He was trying his best to keep it together 'cause his mama was dying. The family was relying on him. Then that Ivy girl found out he was back and decided she wanted him back."

Charlotte closed her eyes. When she had found Ivy, she always knew that it would turn out to be a tragedy, but she had no idea what twists and turns she would encounter. Her heart bled for the young lovers.

"Then she went missing, and the whole town turned on him," James said angrily. "Never mind the fact that he was missing too."

"And they never found him?"

Charlotte phrased her words as a question, but she already knew the answer.

"He was dead," James said simply.

"What?" Charlotte asked in surprise.

James held out his hand for the photo box, and she gave it to him. He searched through it until he found one. It was yellowing and had curled edges.

"Here," James said, handing it to her.

She took it and held back a gasp. It was Martin Baker. He had James's soft brown eyes, and his face radiated confidence. Charlotte could see what had caused

Ivy to fall in love so deeply. He looked handsome in his Army uniform as he stared beyond the camera.

"His mama died a few weeks later," James explained. "Now, you're telling me that that boy clawed his way out of a loony bin to be by her side but couldn't be bothered to turn up when she died? Even in a disguise? He would've shown himself to his only sister at the very least. There's no way he would have left her to fend for herself like that. Ain't no way. Martin Baker died around the same time as Ivy, you mark my words."

CHAPTER SEVEN

"*I* must say, I admire what you're doing," Nat said as they sat at her desk.

Sometimes, Nat forgot the rest of the world existed, and her friends had to reach out to her to bring her back. Her work at the lab was demanding, and she tended to get drawn into her work to the detriment of her personal life. Between the two of them, Charlotte was the more outgoing person, which felt strange.

She felt responsible for Nat and always felt guilty if she neglected her friend. Especially since Nat didn't call or text unless prompted. It was one of the biggest reasons why Nat and Brandon had gotten divorced. Most people eventually gave up on being Nat's friend, but Charlotte had known Nat since they were children. Nat wasn't malicious; she was a good friend in most ways. She just hadn't figured out how to relate to the outside world.

"Really?" Charlotte asked wryly. "I would have thought you'd try to talk me out of this."

Nat took a bite of her salad and chewed slowly. "Most people try to talk me out of things all the time. When I wanted to become a medical examiner instead of any other kind of doctor, everyone tried to talk me out of it. You stuck with me the whole time. So, if you tell me that you want to solve a century-old murder, who am I to stop you?"

"It's different," Charlotte said dully.

"Is it?" Nat asked in confusion. "Have I missed something? Do you not want to solve the murder?"

"No, I do," Charlotte assured her. "It's just...you fit here. You knew what you wanted to do and that it would make you happy. I'm not sure if this is the right thing for me to do. I have so much going on, you know, emotionally. I can't help but wonder if this is just a way for me to avoid how I really feel about my grandmother's death."

Nat shrugged. "It's a conundrum. I knew what I wanted to do because it made me happy. And I was good at it. It never made sense to do something I wasn't as good at or that would make other people happy."

"You have a way of seeing through all the complications," Charlotte said.

"Nonetheless, I admire you," Nat said, digging through her salad with her plastic fork. "It takes courage to embark on a new challenge, and you're taking on several new challenges at once. Maybe you are avoiding something, but you're doing good while you're at it. Besides, this is how I got over my mother's death. I buried myself in work. Maybe I'm not the person you should be talking to about this."

Charlotte took a deep breath. Talking to Nat could be tricky, especially since she didn't always realize how her words could be interpreted.

"Do you not want me to talk to you?" Charlotte asked carefully.

"I like it when you talk to me, but it sounds like you need advice, and I'm not equipped to help you. In a few months, you might realize that you should have taken a different course of action."

"I'll take your advice with a pinch of salt," Charlotte promised, smiling to herself. "How is Amy doing?"

Nat stared at her salad before putting it down. "She's a mix of me and Brandon, but it seems she takes more after Brandon. I don't always know what she needs from me, and it frustrates us both. She prefers being with him."

There was an impossible sadness in Nat's voice. She spoke tonelessly, but Charlotte could pick it up. Nat was able to distance herself emotionally from any situation. The more detached she seemed, the more she cared deep down.

"She loves you," Charlotte assured her.

"Yes, in the way all children love their mothers," Nat said with a shrug, "but I don't think she likes me very much."

"Have you tried showing her this world of yours?" Charlotte asked, gesturing at the lab.

"I can't bring a child here," Nat said with a frown. "Besides, Brandon would hate it."

"Yes, but Amy is old enough to choose where she wants to be," Charlotte pointed out, "and you two are divorced."

Nat seemed to consider it but she shook her head. "My life is easier when he isn't upset."

Charlotte fought her frustration and took a few deep breaths. "I see your point," she said slowly, "but Amy needs to see what consumes your time, otherwise she might assume that you're avoiding her. If you let her understand you, then maybe things would be easier between you."

Nat bit her bottom lip nervously.

"Okay, how about this?" Charlotte asked. "I'm

heading to the library today to find some records from the 1920s. Why don't you two join me? She's a bright kid, and there's no dead bodies involved."

Charlotte wanted to help Nat and get her out of the lab. It seemed like a good idea to involve Amy too. Nat was clearly struggling.

"I'll call her," Nat said, "but she might not want to come."

"Give it a shot," Charlotte urged.

Nat nodded and quickly dialed Amy's number. It was a Saturday, so school wouldn't be a problem. Amy picked up and Nat hurried away to talk to her daughter, leaving Charlotte to finish her own salad.

About a minute later, Nat walked back with a bewildered expression on her face.

"She said yes," Nat said, almost breathlessly. "She sounded excited."

"Your daughter wants to spend time with you," Charlotte said with a smile. "I'm sure she's thrilled that you're reaching out."

Nat smiled as she continued eating.

"I've got to go," Charlotte said. "I need to drop some supplies off at the house before I head to the library. Isla asked me to get some groceries for dinner tonight. Do you mind meeting me there?"

"I don't mind," Nat said, still smiling. "I told Amy to meet us there at three."

After Charlotte left the lab, she headed over to the town's only stationery store. It was a sad excuse for a store as it only had some arts and crafts supplies, none of which she needed. Instead, she got a few sheets of paper and some glue, then decided to order the rest online. Her errands were finished quickly, and she found herself thinking about Ivy and Martin while she shopped.

It was getting tougher to do anything since there was such a shortage of information and clues. Charlotte hated not knowing what had happened—it was like trying to build a puzzle that was missing several pieces.

As she was pulling into her house, she spotted the ugly gnome in the middle of her driveway.

"Are you kidding me?" Charlotte asked in exasperation.

She got out of the car and walked over to it.

"This isn't funny!" she called out.

She looked around, but no one was listening. As she was about to take the gnome back, a thought occurred to her. She smiled mischievously and walked over to her car. All she needed was a sheet of paper, some glue, and a marker.

Charlotte checked one last time to make sure no one

was around then wrote, "KEEP YOUR STUPID GNOME IN YOUR YARD!!!!" It was childish, but it brought a smile to her face. When she was done, she smothered the back of the paper in glue and stuck it to the front of the gnome. Once she was sure it was firmly stuck, she put it in front of her neighbor's yard.

By the time she met Nat and Amy at the library, she was feeling a lot better about life in general. Roma and Archimedes were with her. Charlotte was trying to take Archimedes to more places in an effort to get the over-weight cat to exercise more.

"I like your cats," Amy said as Charlotte got out of the car and the cats hopped out too.

Archimedes meowed loudly in protest then flopped right on the ground.

"Thanks," Charlotte said as she picked Archimedes up. "They're a lot of trouble, but I still love them."

Roma ran straight up to Amy and began rubbing herself between Amy's legs, causing the young teenager to laugh. Amy was only about thirteen years old with strawberry-blonde hair, green eyes, and a smattering of freckles across her nose. She wore a graphic T-shirt and pink cutoffs. It was a sweetly innocent look.

"What would you like us to help you do?" Nat asked, standing awkwardly near Amy.

"Yeah, my mom told me you're trying to solve a

murder," Amy said, her face brightening with anticipation.

"It's probably not as exciting as it sounds," Charlotte said with a chuckle. "Apparently, the library has records dating back to the early 1900s; I'm hoping we can find something about Ivy in there. Do you know how to use a microfiche machine?"

"A what?" Amy asked, scrunching her nose in confusion.

Charlotte chuckled and led them into the library. It was a beautiful wood building in the middle of town. The structure used to be a schoolroom, but it had been transformed into a library in the sixties. Unfortunately, most of its budget went to its upkeep so its technology was straight out of the nineties.

"My friends won't believe me when I tell them what I did this weekend," Amy said as they carried boxes out from the records' room.

The librarian had given them free access to the microfiche machine while she attended her book club.

"Do you get to do this kind of thing everyday, Mom?" Amy asked, looking over at her mother.

"No," Nat said, "I mostly work in the lab."

"You know what's cool about your mom's job?" Charlotte asked as she checked through the records. "She helps the police solve crimes."

"I know," Amy said proudly. "I wrote a report on it last year and got an A."

"You did?" Nat asked in surprise. "Why didn't I hear about it?"

"You were working on a big case or something. I think it was about some strangler who was loose in Boston."

"Another one?" Charlotte sighed, shaking her head slowly.

"I'm sorry I missed it," Nat said with a frown.

"Don't worry, Mom," Amy said, patting Nat's hand. "You're busy. Besides, Dad helped me."

Charlotte took some microfiche out of the box and squinted at it before loading it into the machine. She didn't miss the troubled expression on Nat's face, but chose to look at the screen in an effort to give Nat some space. The newspaper detailed Ivy's disappearance and the search efforts being carried out to find her.

"Did that Martin guy kill her?" Amy asked, reading over Charlotte's shoulder.

"They thought so," Charlotte said thoughtfully, "but I'm not so sure."

"I watched a true crime show the other day, and they said it's almost always the boyfriend who kills the victim," Amy said seriously. "Were they having any problems?"

"That's a very insightful question," Nat said, squinting at the newspaper.

"Don't tell Dad," Amy said wryly. "He thinks I'm too young to be watching that kind of thing."

"Martin was the boyfriend," Charlotte said, "but Elias Rivera was the fiancé."

She took the microfiche out and put the next one in.

"Is that Elias?" Amy asked, gesturing at Ivy and Elias's engagement announcement.

"Yeah," Charlotte said, enlarging the announcement.

Ivy was standing next to Elias in the photo, and they both were staring at the camera. Their arms were linked, and Charlotte thought they made a stunning couple. There was only one problem.

"Boy, she doesn't look happy," Amy said with a grimace.

CHAPTER EIGHT

*A*s Charlotte pulled into her driveway, she was stopped by an infuriating sight. Her neighbor had placed the ugly gnome right in the middle of the driveway with a neon-yellow sticky note on its face.

"This is getting insane," Charlotte muttered as she got out of the car and walked up to the gnome.

The sticky note only had one word on it. *No.*

"No?" Charlotte cried out. "What do you mean no?"

She shook the gnome in the direction of her neighbor's house. It was getting a little ridiculous, and she considered just throwing the gnome in the trash and being done with it. And yet…the thought of giving up didn't sit right with her. The neighbor was the one in the wrong; why did they keep trying to pawn the ugly gnome off on her?

"Oh-ho, this is so far from over, buddy," Charlotte said, walking over to the neighbor's fence. She looked around thoughtfully before finding a nearby bush and stashing the gnome behind it. "Let's see you find this!"

When she got back to her car, she found that she was smiling gleefully.

"What are you smiling at?" Isla asked when Charlotte walked into the house.

"Nothing," Charlotte said, pursing her lips. "I was thinking of a funny joke I heard the other day. How's your day been?"

"It's been great," Isla said with an excited grin. "I walked past your laptop earlier, and I kept hearing these notification sounds, so I checked it out…"

"Are you confessing to snooping around in my stuff?" Charlotte asked, feeling torn between amusement and indignation.

"I thought something was wrong," Isla said with a shrug. "In all the years I've known you, you've never gotten that many messages before."

"Well, that makes me feel unpopular," Charlotte grumbled, scratching the back of her head.

"You're an introvert, and I love you." Isla reached out and patted Charlotte's hand.

"You make being an introvert sound like terminal cancer," Charlotte said, crossing her arms over her chest.

"I do not," Isla said, gasping dramatically. "Anyway, you should probably check your social media. I think you'll be pleased."

"Can't you just tell me what you saw?" Charlotte asked, but she was already heading to the library.

In the few days that she'd been living in the mansion, she had made herself at home in the library. It now functioned as both a workshop for her bookbinding and an office.

"That would defeat the purpose of surprising you," Isla said with a shrug. "You know how much I love surprises."

"I hate surprises. This is more for you, isn't it?"

"My, my, someone's feeling grouchy today," Isla said, raising an eyebrow.

Charlotte picked up her laptop, and to her surprise, she saw hundreds of notifications.

"Whoa," Charlotte said, her eyes widening. "This is insane! Hundreds of people watched my last video. It's almost at three thousand views now!"

"Only three thousand?" Isla asked, peeking over Charlotte's shoulder. "With all that noise I thought you'd at least be over ten thousand."

"Three thousand is a lot!" Charlotte insisted. "If three thousand people came flooding in here, you'd be overwhelmed." She placed the laptop back on the desk and sat down.

"Okay, but three thousand people and three thousand views are completely different," Isla pointed out.

While they spoke, Archimedes sauntered over and flopped down by Charlotte's feet. He began playing with her shoelaces. It was a common occurrence. Whenever he wanted attention, he would always start by playing with her shoelaces, and if she didn't pick him up after a few minutes, he would drape himself dramatically over her feet until she got the hint.

"You know what? You're being cynical. I'm actually very proud of this," Charlotte said, picking Archimedes up and propping him up on her lap. He stretched and put his paws on her shoulder so that he could look at the world behind her.

"You're right," Isla said, holding her hands up in surrender. "I'm sorry, I sound like such a snob. What are you going to do with your newfound fame?"

"I don't know. I'll probably have to run for president or something. Otherwise, my dedicated fanbase might riot."

Isla chuckled good-naturedly. "I hope you're not too high and mighty to take Kenan's stuff back to him. He sent someone over to ask when you'd be done with it."

"What? Are we living in the dark ages or something?

Why didn't he just give me a call?" Charlotte asked, scrunching her nose.

"The guy's weird, and I'm not going to say anything more than that." Isla held her hands up as if to excuse herself from the situation. "He probably wants to get it back before Annette gets her hands on it."

"I thought that when you said they were working together it meant that they were actually getting along," Charlotte said as she stroked Archimedes' back.

"Are you kidding?" Isla asked incredulously. "No way. The longer this project drags on, the closer she gets to murdering him."

"That's weird. Why don't they just stop working together?"

"They're the only two people who care that much about town history," Isla said with a shrug. "I guess they're both each other's necessary evil. Although, to be honest, the feud mostly seems to stem from Annette. Kenan's closely related to some of the most important people in this town's history. It's more than just displays and stories to him. Sometimes Annette can forget that."

Charlotte bit her bottom lip thoughtfully. She felt sorry for Kenan. It probably wasn't pleasant when people felt like they were entitled to his family's history.

"I'm sure Kenan's been handling it well," Charlotte said reasonably, "and Annette's just…passionate."

"Annette's something, all right," Isla said, raising her eyebrows, "but I don't know if I'd describe it as passionate."

Charlotte suppressed a smile and got out of her seat. Archimedes grunted in complaint, so she put him down on the floor. He gave her a long, serious look before walking over to a nearby patch of sunlight.

"I should head over there now," Charlotte said, stretching tiredly. "That way I can get home sooner and be done with this day."

"Was it a tough one?" Isla asked with a grimace.

"No," Charlotte said with a shrug, "I just like being in my pajamas."

Isla rolled her eyes. "Whatever. Hey, what happened with the whole gnome saga? Did you finally break down and just throw the thing away?"

"Something like that," Charlotte said nonchalantly as she walked away.

Once she was out of the library, she allowed herself to smile. Charlotte collected all of Ivy's old things and drove over to Kenan's house. This time, the security guard let her in without any trouble.

Unfortunately, no one came outside to greet her so she balanced the box in her hands as she rang the doorbell with her elbow. After a few minutes of waiting, she was about to give up when a harried maid answered the door.

"Hi," Charlotte said, "I'm here to drop off some of Ivy's things. Kenan let me look through them."

"Oh, thanks," the maid said, reaching out for the boxes.

As she took them, a booming voice came from inside.

"Janeen!" a man shouted. "You'd better be done with the floors!"

Charlotte peeked inside. The house was just as gorgeous on the inside as it was on the outside. It was hard to believe that anyone lived like that.

"I...have to go..." Janeen said, struggling with the unwieldy box as she tried to close the door.

"Are you okay?" Charlotte asked in concern.

"No," Janeen said, looking over at Charlotte.

Her hair was falling into her face, and her uniform was askew. Unlike in the movies, she was wearing a pair of khaki pants and a light-blue golf shirt instead of a white-and-black dress.

"I still have a thousand things to do before the end of the day," Janeen said. "This is a new job, so if I mess it up..."

"You won't mess up," Charlotte assured her

hurriedly. "Why don't you let me take the box inside and you go do whatever you need to do?"

"I don't know…" Janeen said hesitantly. "This needs to go all the way back up to the attic. It's on the fourth floor."

"Point me in the right direction, and I'll figure it out," Charlotte said, taking the box from Janeen. "You've got enough on your plate."

"I don't know if this is a good idea," Janeen said, biting her bottom lip nervously. "I don't know you…"

"Kenan trusted me enough to lend me this stuff, and I'll go up quickly. Or, I could do the floors for you."

"You're crazy, you know that?" Janeen asked, obviously trying to stop herself from smiling.

"I guess," Charlotte said with a shrug. "Okay, where does this go?"

Janeen quickly explained to Charlotte how to get to the attic before the man called out again.

"If you don't get those floors done soon, I'll be forced to take disciplinary action against you," the man said in a stern voice.

"That sounds bad; you'd better go," Charlotte said with a grimace.

Janeen winced and ran off. The house was so big that Charlotte felt intimidated, but Janeen's directions turned out to be helpful. As she ascended the stairs and got to the second floor landing, she spotted a portrait of Ivy Stanhope.

"Okay then," Charlotte said, raising an eyebrow.

The portrait depicted Ivy sitting upright in a chair with her voluminous hair pulled back into a stern bun. She had seen pictures of Ivy before, but the portrait was life-sized and seemed to bring Ivy to life. It was a larger version of the portrait in the museum. Her round face and charming hazel eyes seemed eerily familiar to Charlotte.

"I've fallen down the rabbit hole," Charlotte muttered.

She shook her head and hurried up to the attic. Once she got there, she fought the urge to toss the box to one side and flee down the stairs. The attic took up an entire floor and obviously used to be staff rooms. It was dark and smelled like mothballs.

Charlotte had to go up a cramped staircase that suddenly opened up to a massive yet suffocating space. The windows were boarded up, and it was filled with the belongings of the Stanhope family over the years.

There were huge shelves, and everything was organized alphabetically. Charlotte walked around the room looking for Ivy's space. Finally, she found a single empty shelf with Ivy's name on a plastic label. Charlotte put the box on the shelf, noting that it fit perfectly. She was about to leave when she noticed something peculiar.

A small leather box with a gold lock was stuffed behind some sporting equipment. Curiosity got the better of her, and she picked it up. The letters "I.S." were stamped on the front in gold lettering.

"Ivy," Charlotte murmured, running her hand over the aged leather.

Kenan must have forgotten to give it to her when he had given her the rest of Ivy's things. Or maybe he hadn't seen it. As she stood there, she heard an eerie creaking sound coming from the back of the room.

"I'm out of here," Charlotte decided, tucking the box under her arm.

She hurried out of the Stanhope house as if something was chasing her.

CHAPTER NINE

"$\mathcal{D}$o you have time to chat now?" Nat asked.

She was standing on the porch with a bottle of wine and a box of Charlotte's favorite cookies. The weather had cooled dramatically, and it looked like a storm was brewing.

"I always have time for you. Come on in," Charlotte said, opening the door wider. "Is something wrong?"

"No," Nat said, with a shrug. "I realized that the last time you came to me, I spent most of the time whining about my problems."

"You know I don't see it as whining. Come on in. Isla made pasta for dinner before she left."

"Does she have space to take on another client?" Nat asked as they walked into the kitchen. "I could use someone like Isla in my life."

"I don't know if Isla has space for me anymore," Charlotte said with a grimace.

The kitchen was the heart of the house. It was one of the largest spaces in the house and had been renovated several times over the years. When Charlotte was a kid, they'd spend every holiday at the house, and the kitchen was always full of people and cooking food. As a result, it was one of Charlotte's favorite places in the world.

It was a homey room with mahogany cabinets and granite countertops. While it was a little old-fashioned, Charlotte had no plans to change it. The kitchen reminded her too much of her grandmother.

There was a breakfast nook in one corner with a stained-glass window that depicted a rose garden. Nat headed over to the breakfast nook and dropped onto a chair with a sigh as she put the wine down on the table.

"What? Has she said anything?" Nat asked in confusion. "I always thought that Isla loved working here."

"Me too. I guess maybe she just loved working for my grandmother. I heard her talking to someone when I first got here. She mentioned that she wasn't sure how to tell me something. She hasn't told me what it is yet, and I get the feeling that she's avoiding me."

Nat frowned and leaned back in her chair. "You're reading too much into this."

"Do you think so?" Charlotte asked as she put the pasta in the microwave.

"Yes, you don't know what she wants to tell you, so you assumed that it was bad. Sometimes a gut feeling comes in handy when you're working on something like the Ivy Stanhope case. Other times, it just gets in the way. You know, I once tried to plan a surprise party for Brandon. He accused me of cheating on him."

"I remember that," Charlotte said with a grimace. "He was so paranoid that he accused you right before you told him about the party. We were all hiding in the kitchen, and we heard everything."

The microwave dinged.

Nat shook her head in annoyance. "He never did apologize for that. And yet I'm the emotionless robot who wrecked our marriage."

Charlotte didn't say anything as she took the pasta out of the microwave and began dishing up.

"Speaking of the Ivy Stanhope case, have you made any progress?" Nat asked, getting some wine glasses.

"Yeah…" Charlotte said. "Look what I found."

She gestured to the leather box sitting on the kitchen table.

"This belonged to her?" Nat asked, sitting down again as she sipped her wine. "Thanks for the food. It's delicious."

"Thank Isla. She did all the hard work."

"How are you planning on opening this?" Nat asked, examining the box carefully. "Kenan will kill you if you break this."

"I'm not too worried about that," Charlotte said proudly. "You'd be surprised how many of my book-binding tools double as lockpicking tools."

"That's a weird overlap."

Charlotte shrugged as she picked up a leather pouch that contained all her tools. It had been a present from her grandmother. She unfolded the pouch and took out a few items including an awl and a file with a curved edge.

"Do we need to watch a tutorial or something?" Nat asked, but Charlotte shook her head and inserted the tools into the old lock.

She maneuvered the tools thoughtfully for a few minutes before the lock clicked open.

"I'm impressed, but now I'm also worried about how you obtained such a skillset," Nat asked, raising her eyebrows.

"It's nothing dramatic," Charlotte said with a chuckle. "I always lose my keys somehow, so I thought that this would be a useful skill. Each lock is different, but the fundamentals haven't let me down yet."

"Wouldn't it be easier to just keep track of your keys?" Nat asked in amusement.

Charlotte shrugged. "Maybe, but now I know how to pick a lock, so who needs a key?"

"Your mind is a strange place," Nat commented before taking a bite of pasta. "This is delicious. Did she make the bolognese sauce from scratch?"

"I don't think she knows that you can make it from a packet," Charlotte admitted.

While they spoke, the wind picked up outside and began blowing fiercely. Roma shot inside with a panicked expression and hid behind the refrigerator.

Charlotte sighed. "Poor cat. She's afraid of the storm."

"Never mind the cat," Nat said, inspecting the box carefully, "I want to know what's inside here. Imagine, we might be the first people to look inside this since Ivy went missing."

"I can't ignore the cat," Charlotte protested as she went over to the fridge. "Here, kitty, kitty…"

She got on her hands and knees and tried to entice the cat, but Roma squeezed herself further behind the fridge and watched Charlotte with wide eyes. At that moment, Archimedes walked into the kitchen and began meowing insistently.

"The fat one wants to eat," Nat said, looking over at

Charlotte as she continued inspecting the outside of the box.

"He's not fat," Charlotte said, getting up and stroking Archimedes' ears. "He's cuddly."

"He can't understand me so it's not as if I'm being offensive," Nat pointed out.

"You're offending me," Charlotte said, pulling a face at Nat which Nat ignored.

"I want to know what's inside," Nat said, holding the box up meaningfully.

"So do I," Charlotte said soothingly, "but if I don't feed him then he's only going to cry more. Besides, it's his dinner time. How would you feel if I didn't feed you?"

Nat shrugged as she took a bite of pasta. "I think it would be more tragic if Isla refused to feed me."

"Rude," Charlotte said, rolling her eyes.

Charlotte quickly fed the cats and to her relief, Roma came out from behind the fridge as soon as she heard the sound of her dinner being put into a bowl. By the time she was done, it had already started raining outside.

"You might have to spend the night," Charlotte said as she watched the rain come down in torrents.

"It might stop. Can we open the box now? It feels like my head might explode."

"Gross," Charlotte teased as she opened the box.

It was the size of a small suitcase and was filled with some old makeup, perfume, and a music box. Charlotte felt a stab of disappointment. She had been hoping that it contained the key to unlocking the mystery of Ivy's death. What were they supposed to do with old makeup?

"Do you think we could use some of this?" Nat asked, opening a bright-red compact with golden edgings.

The powder inside was so hard that it looked fossilized.

"I think you'd get the rash of a lifetime," Charlotte said with a grimace.

"You want to know the cool thing about this?" Nat asked. "There's a secret compartment at the bottom for pills or cigarettes or whatever."

She quickly popped the bottom open, and a few white pills fell out. Charlotte picked them up and noticed that the pills had turned slightly yellow with age.

"What do you think this is?" Charlotte asked.

Nat sniffed them and broke a small piece off before pressing it to her tongue. The taste caused her to grimace. "Morphine. Your girl must have been in serious pain at some point."

"Do you think she was addicted?" Charlotte asked in horror.

"We didn't find any traces in her system, so I don't think so," Nat said reasonably, "but she might have had surgery or something at some point. I didn't find any injuries after an initial search, but I'm going to try and get the body back for a deeper examination."

"Why?" Charlotte asked curiously.

"There's something off about the body. I didn't get much time with Ivy since they just wanted me to determine her identity. I think that if I got a second look then I'd be able to come up with more. Look, I don't want to get your hopes up, but I have a sneaking suspicion that I need to look into."

Charlotte wanted to press for more information, but Nat wasn't one to let herself be pressured into anything before she was ready.

"You know," Charlotte said, deciding to change the subject, "I wonder if there's anything else in here that might have a false bottom or secret compartment."

"That's not a bad idea," Nat said, perking up. "Here, I'll check the rest of the makeup."

Charlotte took the big leather box and began feeling around for a latch or button of some kind. When she didn't find anything, she moved on to the music box. It was a gorgeous carved wooden box that played Debussy's "Clair de Lune" when it was opened. A wooden ballerina with a tulle skirt twirled around the box as the music played.

As Charlotte looked at the box, she realized that the space inside was small compared to how big it was. She began feeling around cautiously when she spotted a small latch hidden behind the ballerina's gears.

"I think I found something," Charlotte said as she lifted the latch.

The bottom opened with a click, and a leather-bound journal fell out of the bottom of the box.

Nat's eyes widened. "Is that…?"

"Ivy's diary," Charlotte said.

She opened the book to find Ivy's sloping cursive.

"What does it say?" Nat asked.

"She's talking about getting engaged to Elias," Charlotte explained as she read. "Apparently, she didn't think it was a good idea, but Kingsley was all for it. Elias had several business connections that would benefit them."

"I don't know why, but this Kingsley guy gives me the creeps," Nat said with a shudder.

"I think he was misguided, but Ivy trusted him implicitly," Charlotte said. "Here, listen to this… 'I would not go against my heart so lightly, if not for my high regard for dear Kingsley. He's been a wonder during these trying months, and I know he has my best interests at heart.'"

"Well, that's something," Nat said. "I suppose they were close because of how they grew up. Besides, Ivy didn't have anyone else at that point. Maybe she figured that Elias was a good enough choice."

"This is strange," Charlotte said with a frown. "Everything I've heard about Ivy so far gave me the impression that she was a strong, fiery person. This makes me think that she was meek and pliable."

"Maybe people built up this idea of her in their head. It's possible that Ivy was nothing like everyone thinks."

"I guess," Charlotte said, feeling a little disappointed.

The two of them took turns reading Ivy's diary as the storm raged outside. They ate their pasta and enjoyed the wine as they read Ivy's account of the last few weeks of her life. Her writing was sporadic, and she didn't seem to have much of an interest in what was happening around her. However, things changed the closer they got to the end of the diary.

"Martin came back," Charlotte said, sitting up straighter when she read the last entry. "And that's not all… She was scared."

"What?" Nat asked in confusion. "Why?"

"I don't know," Charlotte said. "She just says that she's frightened of running into him again. It's dated two days before she disappeared. And look…the last page has been ripped out."

CHAPTER TEN

at ended up spending the night, and they spent most of it talking about what could have happened to the last page of the diary.

"I think the most frustrating part about this is that it could have happened any time in the past hundred years, and no one would know," Charlotte said at breakfast the next morning.

"Ivy could even have ripped it out herself," Nat said with a shrug as she ate her cereal.

"This is so frustrating." Charlotte sighed as Roma played with the empty cereal box. "I mean, it's like starting a puzzle and knowing that I probably won't find all the pieces. I'm supposed to live the rest of my life knowing that I might not know everything that happened."

"It's probably how Annette feels," Nat pointed out.

"Way to make me feel guilty about this," Charlotte muttered.

"I'm not trying to make you feel guilty. Technically, you've done nothing wrong. After all, why isn't she trying to find out who killed Ivy?"

"She might be," Charlotte said defensively. "Maybe she's keeping it quiet too. Or maybe she's got too much work with the town museum to think about that right now."

"When I heard that a body had been found in the well, I fully expected Annette to come banging down my door," Nat said, shaking her head. "You know she tried to make the police coerce Kenan Stanhope into giving her full access to his family's belongings? Brandon told me all about it when we were still civil with each other."

"I wasn't aware that you were ever civil with one another," Charlotte said with a chuckle.

"That was low," Nat said, wagging her finger at Charlotte. "Anyway, I was super surprised when you ended up banging on my door for more information."

"I did not bang on your door," Charlotte said, her cheeks turning red.

"Maybe not, but you were pretty insistent. Don't get me wrong, it was a surprise. I think you're coming out of your shell. I didn't expect that to happen so quickly.

You're one of the best people I know, but it usually takes you a while to warm up to a new situation."

Charlotte squirmed uncomfortably in her seat. She looked over at where Roma was playing. The cat had wormed her way into the cereal box and was busy ripping apart the bottom of the box.

"I suppose this whole thing has forced me to put myself out there," Charlotte said thoughtfully.

"Have you been outside yet?" Isla walked into the kitchen unexpectedly. She stopped short when she saw Nat. "Oh, hey, Nat. How's it going?"

"Great. Charlotte fed me some of your pasta last night. It was delicious."

"That's great to hear," Isla beamed. "I'm always flattered when people like my cooking. Anyway, have either of you been outside yet?"

"What do you think?" Charlotte asked, gesturing to their pajamas.

"No, I didn't think so," Isla said, putting her hands on her hips as she looked at them.

As always, she looked effortlessly beautiful in her blue jeans, white button-up shirt, and raincoat.

"You need to see this," Isla said, grabbing Charlotte's hand.

Charlotte yelped as Isla pulled her to her feet. Since she didn't have much of a choice, she allowed herself to be dragged outside. The storm had done a number on the yard, and there were broken branches, leaves, and debris lying all around.

"Whoa," Nat said, walking out behind Charlotte and Isla. "That's a huge mess."

Charlotte sighed. "We're going to need to hire a gardening service to help us with this. Great, I'm going to have to spend more money that I don't have."

"Don't worry about that," Isla said, shaking her head in annoyance. "I've got contacts who can help us out. No, I'm talking about that." She pointed at the ugly gnome that was sitting on the walkway in front of the house.

"That's the ugliest thing I've ever seen in my life," Nat said with a shudder. "How did it stay upright when everything else blew over."

"I'll tell you how," Charlotte said with a huff as she walked up to the gnome. "My neighbor insists on doing this. They probably found where I hid the stupid thing and think they're being clever."

There was another bright sticky note on the gnome's face. *Nice try.*

"Why can't we just throw the thing away?" Isla asked. "I don't think the principle of the thing or whatever is worth all this back and forth. You're going to run out of sticky notes."

"This is personal," Charlotte said, shaking her head. "They had to come onto the property to plant this thing here. That's trespassing! We're obviously dealing with a criminal."

Nat and Isla exchanged a worried look before looking back at Charlotte in disbelief.

"Okay, fine," Charlotte said sheepishly, "maybe that's taking it too far. I'm not giving up though. What kind of entitled jerk sneaks onto another person's yard so early in the morning?"

"Didn't you hide it in their bush?" Isla asked incredulously.

"You know what?" Charlotte asked. "I'm going to end this whole thing right now."

She marched into the house and went to the library. Once she got what she needed, she went back outside.

"I thought you were throwing it away," Isla spluttered when Charlotte walked out of the house with the gnome tucked into the crook of her arm.

"Oh, no way!" Charlotte said. "I figured out a way to straighten this out once and for all."

"I don't believe you!" Isla called out before walking back into the house.

"I've never seen this vindictive side of your personality before," Nat said, hurrying to catch up to Charlotte.

"I'm not being vindictive," Charlotte protested. "I'm just standing up for myself."

Nat scrunched up her forehead as she thought, then she shook her head. "No, I don't see how this translates to you standing up for yourself. It's weird. And a little vindictive."

"Fine," Charlotte said, "it may be a little vindictive. I don't know why I don't want to give this up, but I can't."

"May I tell you what I think?" Nat asked.

"You don't have to ask," Charlotte said, walking up the neighbor's driveway until she got to their gate.

She looked around to make sure that no one was looking before she knelt to the ground and began applying superglue to the gnome's base.

"I think you're enjoying this," Nat said. "You got a taste of mystery with this whole Ivy Stanhope case, but it's lacking a certain element of excitement so you're using this to compensate."

Charlotte frowned as she held the gnome in place. "I guess it makes sense, but I have another explanation."

"What's that?" Nat asked as Charlotte stood up.

"I have an entitled jerk for a neighbor, and now I'll have won this little competition," Charlotte said with a smile.

As she spoke, a car drove up to the driveway. All

Charlotte saw was that the car was blue and that it was probably her neighbor.

"Let's go!" Charlotte cried.

Nat didn't need more prompting and took off running. They both ran as fast as they could as the neighbor got out of the car.

"Hey!" he protested as they ran away, but they didn't stop until they were safely in the house.

"Do you think he's going to come over here?" Nat asked as Charlotte slammed the front door shut.

"I'll tell him that he shouldn't have started it," Charlotte said as she leaned against the closed door.

"What's going on?" Isla asked, rushing into the foyer.

Nat and Charlotte exchanged a glance before breaking out into laughter. Isla stood there with a bewildered expression on her face, which only made them laugh harder.

"You two are being very childish," Isla said with a sigh.

"I'm sorry," Nat said, chortling. "I suppose this is an immature way to spend the morning."

"Don't be too harsh on us, Isla," Charlotte said. "The past few months have been extremely stressful. Let us blow off some steam."

"I'm all for blowing off steam," Isla said. "You can

take a vacation or take up a new hobby. Stop terrorizing the neighbors."

With that, she walked out of the room. Nat and Charlotte looked at each other again and started chuckling.

A few hours later, Charlotte was working on another bookbinding project. The work helped to clear her head which allowed her to think about the case. As she worked, she couldn't escape the feeling that Annette would be able to help with her situation. Besides, Annette had worked hard to preserve Ivy's memory. Didn't she deserve some input in the investigation?

The more she worked, the more convinced she became that she needed to go see Annette. Finally, she couldn't take it anymore and threw on her jacket.

"Where are you going?" Isla asked as Charlotte walked past.

"I need to see Annette about something."

"Do you really have to go?" Isla asked, scrunching up her nose. "I always try to avoid Annette unless it's absolutely necessary."

"I might regret it, but this is something I feel I have to do," Charlotte said with a shrug. "I'll see you later, okay? Could you keep an eye on Roma and Archimedes?"

Isla nodded and Charlotte smiled gratefully. When

she got outside, she noted with trepidation that the sky was dark with rain clouds. It looked like they were in for another storm.

She made up her mind to get back home before the storm broke. When she got to the museum, she was surprised to find that the door was locked.

"Hello?" Charlotte called, tugging on the handles.

Nothing.

She tried knocking, but nothing happened. As she was about to leave, she heard a crash coming from inside. Charlotte considered leaving, but something didn't feel right. Instead, she walked around the old building and found a back door.

"You're imagining things. Just go home," Charlotte murmured to herself.

Instead of turning back, she tested the door handle and found that it jumped open under her touch.

"Hello?" Charlotte called as she walked into the dark building.

Overhead, thunder boomed in the sky and a cold wind started blowing. Charlotte shivered as she walked in. As she made her way to the front room, she heard footsteps scuffing on the wooden floor.

"Is anyone here?" Charlotte asked, freezing by the door. "Annette? Is that you?"

She didn't want to go further, and a shiver ran down

her spine. Something was definitely up. Annette would have answered Charlotte if she was there. Charlotte saw someone moving in the dark, and she felt along the wall for the light switch. As she was about to flip the switch, someone barreled right into her, knocking her to the floor.

"Hey!" she cried as she fell to the floor. Her head hit the wall, and she leapt to her feet in case the person tried to do something else.

By the time she was on her feet, the person was already out of the building. Charlotte groaned and turned on the light. She would have to get Annette's number to warn her that something weird had happened. As she was about to leave, she spotted something chilling.

Someone was lying by one of the display stands. All she saw was a hand, but she knew something was wrong. Charlotte felt a rising horror as she walked over and saw Annette lying on the floor, her eyes staring sightlessly at the ceiling.

CHAPTER ELEVEN

*C*harlotte wished that her hands would stop shaking. She was sitting in a police car while they searched the scene. An ambulance had come to take Annette away. She could have told them that Annette didn't need an ambulance.

It was the second time she had found a body, and it felt so much worse than the first. There had been something sickening about finding a human skeleton, but finding a person she had known would haunt her nightmares.

She hugged herself tightly as she sat in the back of the car. The police had been nice to her, but she couldn't help but be wary around them. Did they think that she was guilty? They had seemed to take her seriously when she told them about the person who'd knocked her over.

However, she wasn't sure that they believed her. She was well aware how her story sounded.

When Brandon walked over to her with a serious expression, she felt like throwing up. There was no way she could go to prison for something she didn't do. She cursed herself for not leaving well enough alone. Instead of staying at home where it was safe, she had gotten herself into a massive mess.

The storm had started sometime after Charlotte called 911, and it was pouring with rain as Brandon made his way over to her.

When he got into the car, he turned to look at her with a grim expression. His hair was soaking wet and stood up in spikes. Brandon had unassuming looks and could easily blend into a crowd. He didn't stand out in any way, but he had a keen eye for detail and often used his chameleon-like abilities to his advantage. Sometimes his commanding officer had him dress up in plain clothes and sit in a jail cell when they brought in an uncooperative criminal. Usually, Brandon managed to get them to spill their secrets in minutes.

"You want to talk about what happened?" he asked gently.

"I already told you what happened," Charlotte said, watching him carefully. "I came here—"

"Right, to tell Annette that you found some interesting information about the Ivy Stanhope murder," Brandon said.

She could hear the skepticism in his voice. Her shoulders slumped, and she looked out the window thoughtfully.

"Come on, Charlotte," he said kindly, "it doesn't need to be like this. Tell me what really happened. As far as I know, you never knew Annette. You don't have any kind of connection with her."

"Ivy Stanhope was found in a well in my grandmother's garden," Charlotte reminded him. "Annette was the town historian. I'm pretty sure that's a connection. Look, I never would have done anything like this. I hate to bring it up, but you've known me for years. You know what kind of person I am."

Brandon watched her carefully before shaking his head. "I want to believe you, Char, I really do."

She bristled at the sound of the nickname. He was the type of person who gave everyone a nickname whether they wanted one or not. She belonged firmly in the latter category.

"It's just that it sounds a little crazy," Brandon continued. "Trust me, I've been in this business for a long time, and the crazy explanations are rarely true."

She hated that about him. He could make anything sound reasonable. Somehow, Brandon was able to take a person's reasoning and turn it on them. When Nat and Brandon were going through their divorce, Nat had spent hours complaining about how Brandon always seemed to twist her words against her. He could have a person believing they were crazy in just one conversation.

"I'll tell you again, ask Isla," Charlotte said gritting her teeth. "I left the house and came straight here. There's no way I could have rushed here and killed Annette. Ask Nat about the time of death; I'm sure that she'll be able to corroborate what I've said."

"That's the thing," Brandon said with a grimace, "since you and Nat are friends, we're going to have to send the body to a different coroner. It's a conflict of interest."

"Oh, but your divorce isn't a conflict of interest?" Charlotte snapped. She knew she was being rude, but her nerves were frayed. "Shouldn't someone else be interrogating me given your and Nat's...complicated... history?"

Brandon leaned back with a wounded expression. "They sent me here to talk to you because we know each other. I thought it would be easier if I came over to talk to you. Look, Char, I'm on your side here. I swear. You need to give me more to work with."

"I wish I could!" Charlotte insisted. "I heard a crash

coming from inside, and when I went around the back, someone crashed into me as they ran out. I didn't get a good look at their face. If I knew what was inside, I would have chased after him."

"It was a him?" Brandon asked quickly, narrowing his eyes at her.

She nodded quickly. "He was at least a foot taller than me. And he had his head turned away from me, otherwise I would have seen his face."

"Great," Brandon said, "we've got a gender and height. Actually, he could have been wearing inserts so we can't go off of that."

"Sounds tough," Charlotte said with a grimace. "Sorry."

Brandon gave her a searching look before shaking his head.

"I heard you spent the day with Amy," Brandon said quietly.

"What does that have to do with anything?" Charlotte asked in confusion.

He shrugged and looked away. "She had fun. I wanted to thank you for that. I think she actually connected with her mom for the first time in a while. You're a good influence on Nat. You always knew how to get through to her. I wish I had that ability."

Charlotte didn't say anything. She put her hands on

her lap and leaned as far back on the backseat as she could. The conversation was making her uncomfortable. They were going into dangerous territory, and she didn't want to betray Nat in any way.

"Am I going to be arrested or something?" she asked eventually in a small voice.

Brandon snapped out of his thoughts and looked over at her. "I don't see why we should arrest you. Just know that if you've been lying to us then I'm going to find out. And friends or not, I'll throw you in jail so fast it will make your head spin."

Charlotte's chest tightened, and she found it hard to breathe. She nodded breathlessly and tried to focus on getting one breath out after another.

"You're free to leave, but I'll need you to come to the station tomorrow to give me your statement," he said.

She nodded absently and got out of the car. The rain pelted her, but she barely felt it as she went to her car. When she got home, she felt as though she was in a daze. It was hard to think clearly, and when she got to the house, Isla was waiting for her in the foyer.

"Are you okay?" Isla asked, rushing over to her. "Brandon called me and told me what happened."

"Brandon called you?" Charlotte asked with a frown.

"He was worried about you, hon," Isla said, draping a towel around Charlotte's shoulders. "I can't believe this happened again! There's something really weird going on."

"It's like I'm a magnet for death," Charlotte said glumly as she sat on one of the couches.

Archimedes was sitting on the armchair across from her. When he saw her, he meandered over and climbed onto her lap. His warmth meant the world to her, and she stroked his ears lovingly.

"First my grandmother, then Ivy, and now Annette…" Charlotte shook her head. "I think something weird is going on."

"What do you think it is?" Isla asked with a frown.

"I don't know, but I think the killer was looking for something in the museum," Charlotte said. "They must have switched off the lights when I got there, because everything was shut up. They must have closed the blinds to avoid being seen."

"I wonder what Annette had that got her killed," Isla said thoughtfully.

"I don't know, but I want to go find out," Charlotte said resolutely.

"What?" Isla asked in surprise.

"I've come this far, and I won't let the police think that I did this. You weren't there, Isla. Brandon basically threatened me. If they get it into their heads that I killed Annette, then I'm going to be in serious trouble."

"What do you want to do about it?" Isla asked in concern.

"I'm going to sneak into the museum tonight and have a look around," Charlotte said. "Brandon told me that my story sounds crazy, which means that he's going to ignore crucial evidence because he doesn't believe me."

Isla pursed her lips and looked away.

"I know you probably think that it's not a good idea," Charlotte said, wringing her hands. "It's just—"

"No," Isla said, "I think it's a great idea."

"What?" Charlotte asked in surprise.

"We're going to need some gloves," Isla said thoughtfully. "The last thing we need is for the police to find our fingerprints all over the place."

"What do you mean 'we'?" Charlotte asked, feeling bewildered.

"You don't think you're going to do this alone, do you?" Isla scoffed. "No way I'm going to let you have all the fun. Besides, I'm glad you're becoming more adventurous, but you haven't exactly been discreet."

Isla gave Charlotte a meaningful look, and Charlotte grimaced.

"You're talking about the gnome thing, aren't you?"

"Of course, I am," Isla said, throwing her hands up in

frustration. "Who superglues a gnome to someone's driveway?"

"Is it still there?" Charlotte asked curiously.

"You're unbelievable," Isla said, glowering at Charlotte. "Who even does that?!"

"Me?" Charlotte said with a simple shrug. "I don't know if we should be doing this though… It was fine when it was just me, but I don't want to get you into any trouble."

"Don't worry about it," Isla said, waving her hand dismissively. "Okay, so this is what we're going to do…"

They spent the next few hours discussing the case and what they would do moving forward. Charlotte decided that it was best to search the museum when no one else was around, so they waited until midnight before they left the house.

The museum looked eerie in the dark, and Charlotte felt sick to her stomach when she looked at the building.

"I know this is scary, but if you don't face your fear now, then it's only going to get stronger," Isla said, giving Charlotte a side hug.

Charlotte took a deep breath and nodded before walking up to the museum. She picked the front door's lock and walked inside. There was police tape over the door, but they ducked underneath it.

"Is it just me or does this feel spooky?" Isla asked with a shiver.

"Definitely," Charlotte said, avoiding the spot where she had found Annette's body.

They searched through the front room before heading to the rest of the building. There were several little evidence tags all over the place, and Charlotte realized that the police had probably taken everything of value with them. Just as she was about to leave, she found something in Annette's office.

It was a small room that looked more like a broom closet and could only comfortably hold a desk. An antique suitcase was sitting on the desk.

"This must have been what Annette was working on," Isla said, walking up to the desk.

Charlotte looked inside the suitcase and spotted several old garments. A niggling feeling formed in the back of her mind. She picked up one of the dresses and noticed that the initials "I.S." had been embroidered into the inner lining.

As Charlotte dug into the clothes, she found a note folded in between the garments.

You got what you asked for, this is all we have left from that time period. I swear, there's nothing left. Elias didn't keep many of Ivy's things after she disap-

peared. This was obviously a painful time for him. Leave me alone now, I'm serious.

-JH

Charlotte went cold. Had Jacob Haskins delivered the bag himself?

"This belonged to Ivy," Charlotte said with a frown. "This is going to sound crazy, but do you think it's possible that Annette's murder had anything to do with Ivy's?"

"It was a hundred years apart; I don't know how they could have anything in common," Isla said reasonably.

"Maybe, but it's weird that she happened to die when she was going through some of Ivy's things."

"I guess," Isla said with a shrug, "but to be fair, she was always working on this. It could be a coincidence."

"It's a possibility," Charlotte said, feeling a twinge of uncertainty.

"Can we go now?" Isla asked. "This place is giving me the creeps."

"Okay, let's go," Charlotte said, looking at the bag one last time.

They exited the museum without any incident, and Charlotte felt elated that they had pulled it off. Unfortunately, any good feelings faded when they drove up to the house. The car's headlights shone like a spotlight on the bright red words painted on the garage. Some of the lettering was dripping and made it look like the words were painted in blood.

"It's fresh," Charlotte breathed.

She couldn't take her eyes off the threat.

Back off! Leave the dead in peace.
Or you'll join Annette.

CHAPTER TWELVE

"Who would do something like this?" Isla raged, getting out of the car.

"Isla, get back in the car," Charlotte insisted. "The person who did this might still be out there!"

"Oh, I hope they are," Isla scoffed. "You hear that, you coward? Come on out! You think it's funny trying to scare us? I'm calling the police!"

Charlotte looked around anxiously before turning the car off. She got out and walked over to the paint. It was a strange way to threaten someone, and she wondered why they had chosen to add the middle phrase: *Leave the dead in peace.* It would have taken a lot of time to write that, and it took a lot of space. Things were heating up, and she felt close to a breakthrough.

As she walked to the door, she tripped over something in the dark and fell painfully.

"What on earth?" she asked in annoyance.

She put on her phone's flashlight, and there in the middle of her walkway was the ugly gnome.

"You're kidding me!" she cried.

The base was secured to the walkway with cement which was quickly drying. She had knocked it slightly off-kilter when she tripped over it, and the gnome's eyes seemed to mock her as she looked at it.

"What now?" Isla asked, walking over to her.

When she saw the gnome, she crossed her arms over her chest and glared at Charlotte.

"You can't blame this on me," Charlotte said. "I had no idea he'd do something stupid like this."

"What? Stupid like gluing the thing to the driveway?" Isla asked, narrowing her eyes at Charlotte. "Honestly, this has gone on long enough."

"You're missing something very important," Charlotte said. "We couldn't have been gone for longer than an hour. That means that someone painted this on our garage and cemented this thing in place. Look, the cement is wet. Someone obviously did this while we were gone. What if it wasn't two different people?"

"You think the neighbor is threatening you to stay

away from the Ivy Stanhope case?" Isla asked. "I don't know, it seems a little far-fetched."

"As far-fetched as having a feud over a gnome?"

Isla bit the inside of her cheek and looked away. "I called the cops. They said they're sending a squad car over. Let me tell you, this might not help your case."

"They already think I had something to do with Annette's murder," Charlotte said glumly as she pushed the gnome over.

She looked over at the house and saw Roma sitting on the windowsill inside the house. The cat looked curious and was standing on her hind legs as she rested her front paws on the window. It was clear that she wanted to be a part of the action.

While Isla waited for the cops, Charlotte got a trowel out of the house and scraped the cement off the walkway. After all the antics over the past few days, the gnome was looking worse for wear. Its paint was chipping, and the base had been damaged from where her neighbor had removed the gnome from his driveway.

It didn't seem possible, but the gnome was looking a lot uglier. She began thinking of ways to retaliate when the police car raced up the street. Charlotte was impressed by the quick response. Either it was a slow night at the station or they were taking the threat seriously. She hoped it was the latter.

"There you are, Ron," Isla said as a young policeman stepped out of the vehicle.

"I heard there was a disturbance. What's going on?" Ron asked anxiously.

Charlotte wasn't reassured by Ron's appearance. It looked like he had just left high school, and his uniform didn't fit him properly. He was short and stocky with a button nose that made him look very young.

"Someone painted this threat here," Charlotte said, gesturing at the garage door.

Ron nodded and walked over to the garage. He inspected the door for a while, and Charlotte got a sinking feeling as she realized he probably didn't know what he was looking for.

"Were you in the house when this happened?" Ron asked, turning to Isla.

"Not exactly," Isla said carefully. "We went out for a drive…"

"A drive?" Ron asked in confusion. "At this time of the night?"

"I got my period," Charlotte said quickly. "I needed some supplies, and apparently the only thing open around here is the 24-hour convenience mart at the gas station."

Ron's cheeks flushed, and he nodded hurriedly. People rarely looked into an excuse involving menstruation. Charlotte had learned that in high school when she used the excuse to get out of P.E. "Do you have any security cameras? Maybe you caught the person who did this on camera."

"We don't have any cameras, Ron," Isla said patiently. "The only place with security cameras is the bank and the supermarket. We don't have anything worth stealing."

"Okay," Ron said, scratching the back of his neck. "I guess there's nothing more that I can do…"

"What?" Charlotte asked angrily. "Someone vandalized my property! And they threatened to kill me."

"Easy there," Ron said, motioning for her to slow down. "It's probably a prank. People have been talking about how you're trying to solve this murder. Someone probably thought that it would be funny to do something like this."

"It's not funny!" Charlotte said forcefully. "This is a serious threat. At least go talk to my neighbor."

"Your neighbor?" Ron asked in confusion. "Why would I do that?"

"He cemented this gnome onto my walkway around the same time that the threat was painted onto the garage," Charlotte said, holding the gnome out meaningfully. "He could be the person who's threatening me."

"Why would your neighbor threaten you?" Ron

asked carefully. "And why would he cement a lawn gnome to your walkway?"

"Don't get her started," Isla said, shaking her head.

"This is more than just about the stupid gnome!" Charlotte insisted. She quickly told Ron what had happened with the gnome, and by the time she was done talking, he was looking at her in bewilderment.

"Okay," Ron said, "I guess I could talk to him tomorrow…"

"No way," Isla said, shaking her head firmly. "You march over there right now and find out what's going on. Even if he didn't spray-paint our garage, he still might have seen something."

Ron sighed and his shoulders slumped as he got into the car and went over to the neighbor. Charlotte sat on the porch steps as she waited anxiously for Ron to return. Her leg bounced as she chewed on her thumbnail.

"What are we going to do if Ron can't do anything?" Charlotte asked Isla.

"We're not going to give up, if that's what you're thinking," Isla said sternly. "No one gets to march around threatening people like that. Honestly, this is a free country."

"Yes, but doesn't this prove what I was saying earlier?" Charlotte asked. "I seriously think that Annette's murder had something to do with Ivy's murder."

"I'm starting to think that you're right about that," Isla admitted.

It took another ten minutes for Ron to come back. As soon as Charlotte saw him, she knew he didn't have good news for them.

"Your neighbor maintains that while he certainly cemented the gnome to the walkway, he never painted the threat on the garage, and he never saw anyone doing it either. Look, lady, maybe you should stop bothering him; he seems nice."

"He seems nice?" Charlotte protested. "He said he didn't do it so you just believe him?"

"Sure," Ron said with a shrug. "I don't see why he'd lie to me. Look, there's nothing much we can do, okay? Maybe you should take this as a lesson to mind your own business."

Charlotte gaped at him in surprise while Isla jumped to her feet.

"Is that all you have to say for yourself?" Isla asked furiously. "Someone threatened to kill her!"

"Not directly," Ron said with a shrug. "I'm sure it will be fine."

With that, he got back into his car and drove off. Isla grumbled and clenched her fists.

"I can't believe that guy," Isla said.

"I don't think there's anything we can do tonight," Charlotte said as she got to her feet and stared at the threat with a heavy feeling. "Let's call it a night and try again tomorrow. Obviously, the police aren't going to do anything."

"We'll see about that," Isla said, glaring at the road angrily.

Charlotte sighed and guided her inside. "Come on, you can spend the night."

"You're right about that," Isla said. "There's no way I'm leaving you alone tonight."

They went inside and got ready for bed. It was about three in the morning when Charlotte finally got into bed, but she found that sleep eluded her. It was hard to rest when the details of the case kept swirling around her head.

Finally, she got up with a sigh and headed down to the kitchen where she had left Ivy's diary. She couldn't ignore the nagging feeling that she was missing something. Charlotte read through the entire diary, and when she got to the end, she was feeling more frustrated than ever. As she was about to put the book down, she noticed a few threads sticking out the top of the book.

Charlotte turned it around and noticed that the binding was slightly askew. Her breath hitched in her throat in excitement. Someone had removed the binding and glued it back wrong. She hurried to her worktable and carefully removed the binding.

When she separated the leather from the cardboard inside, she spotted a single photograph. It was so thin that it couldn't be felt through the leather binding. The photograph featured a newborn baby wrapped tightly in a blanket, its face scrunched up as it slept. Ivy's familiar sloping writing had written something on the back.

Our precious baby girl. 1919. Martina Baker, adopted by Helen and Royce Baker. I chose them because they shared your surname. I'll love you forever, my darling.

CHAPTER THIRTEEN

*S*ince Charlotte couldn't sleep, she decided to make good use of her time. She found a ladder in the shed and carried it to the fence that separated her yard from her neighbor's yard. It was risky, but she placed it by a large oak tree that hung partially in her yard. She tied the gnome to a branch that hung over his garden.

Once she was done, she climbed down and went back into the house. She hadn't appreciated how Ron had taken the neighbor's side, and it only cemented her idea that he was an entitled jerk. Although a part of her knew that she was judging him unfairly, she was much too sleep deprived and angry to care about being reasonable.

When she was done hanging the gnome in the tree,

she climbed back in bed. A few minutes later, Roma jumped onto the bed and cuddled up to her side. Just as Charlotte was drifting off, Archimedes joined Roma, and the two cats purred together as Charlotte fell asleep.

She managed to sleep deeply, and when she woke up, she was surprised to see that it was nearly noon. As she lay there, trying to gather her thoughts, she remembered what she had found the previous evening. Ivy had given birth a few years before she died.

Charlotte threw the covers to one side, causing Archimedes to meow in protest.

"I'm sorry, baby cat," Charlotte said, stroking him gently. "I forgot that you were lying there."

She took a few minutes to take a shower and get ready for the day. When she hurried down the stairs, she heard Isla singing along to the radio.

"I'm heading out," Charlotte called, "I'll see you later."

"Where are you going?" Isla asked, peeking her head around the doorway.

"I need to see Nat," Charlotte said. "I found something interesting last night, and I need her opinion on it. I'll fill you in when I get back."

"Okay," Isla said. "Although, I should let you know that I went and got some stuff from my house. I'll be staying here for a little while until this all blows over. Don't argue, just let me do this for you."

Charlotte smiled gratefully before heading out the door. When she got to Nat, her friend was pacing her office angrily.

"Hey, what's wrong?" Charlotte asked in surprise.

"Charlotte!" Nat cried before hugging Charlotte tightly. "I heard what happened. Can you believe Brandon tried to keep this from me? I found out about the murder in the newspaper! Why didn't you tell me what happened?"

Charlotte grimaced and quickly told Nat what had happened after she had found Annette's body. While she spoke, Nat walked over to her desk and sat down with an overwhelmed expression.

"All that happened in one day?" Nat asked. "I can't believe it."

"Me neither." Charlotte sighed.

"I wish I could help, but Brandon had the body sent to a different medical examiner. It's frustrating, but I know the other M.E. I think I should send him a message and find out if they know anything. You know, if this has anything to do with Ivy then you might have already met the killer."

"Maybe," Charlotte said as Nat began texting on her phone. "Do you know anyone named Jacob Haskins?"

"I know Jake," Nat said, nodding quickly. "He's a royal jerk, if you ask me."

"How do you know him?" Charlotte asked curiously.

"He's a surgeon down at the hospital and thinks he's God's gift to women. We went on a date after the divorce. My friend set us up because she thought I needed some fun. It was the last time I went on a date. All it did was remind me how awful dating is. He spent the entire time talking about himself and how rich his family is. He even had the audacity to tell me that he wouldn't be buying dinner because he wanted to make sure that I wasn't a gold digger."

As Nat spoke, Charlotte sat down in the chair across from Nat's desk. It was comfortably cushioned, and Charlotte found that she was still exhausted from the day before. She hoped that they found the killer soon so that her life could go back to normal. Charlotte was the type of person who always stuck to her sleep schedule. Her recent string of late nights was taking its toll on her body.

"Gross," Charlotte said, scrunching her nose. "I can't believe the nerve of that guy."

"Why do you want to know about him?" Nat asked with a frown.

"His name keeps popping up in this case," Charlotte admitted. "Annette told me that he's related to Elias Rivera."

"If Elias was anything like Jake then I feel very sorry for poor Ivy," Nat said with a shiver.

"I don't know if being a jerk means he'd be a murderer," Charlotte said. "I don't want to go chasing after everyone who was related to someone that Ivy knew."

"Annette might have done that," Nat pointed out. "It might even be what got her killed. Anyway, I think you should look at Jake more closely. When Brandon found out that I had gone out on a date with Jake, he nearly lost his mind. Apparently, Jake was once arrested for aggravated assault. The charges were dropped after Jake's family made a massive donation to the victim's company."

"Interesting," Charlotte said thoughtfully. "Oh, by the way, there's one more thing that I needed to show you. Look at this."

She slid the photograph across the desk to Nat. Charlotte sat back as she watched Nat pick up the photograph and absorb the implications. To her surprise, Nat merely put the picture down and grimaced.

"Remember how I told you that something seemed off to me about Ivy's remains?" Nat asked. "Well, my colleague got back to me. They managed to put all the bones together and my suspicions were confirmed. Ivy had given birth sometime before she died. Now we know why she had those pills. If she had given birth and they had to operate on her then she would have been in pain for months afterward."

Charlotte leaned back in her chair. The situation was becoming increasingly complicated each day. Annette's murder had signaled that whatever led to Ivy's death still had consequences in their day.

"Nowadays a pregnant woman wouldn't draw much attention," Charlotte said, "but an unmarried pregnant woman in 1919 would have been shocking. She probably met up with Martin while he was on leave, and when he went back to war, she was left with the consequences. She probably thought he was coming back, then when he didn't, she realized that she had to give the baby up for adoption."

"Her parents were dead and she was a wealthy young woman, surely she didn't need to give the baby up?" Nat said with a frown.

"It's more complicated than that," Charlotte said. "She had inherited the entire estate. If her business managers and partners found out what had happened, she would have been blackballed. Even the wealthy didn't escape the consequences of breaking societal convention. Besides, the child would have grown up with the stigma of being a bastard. Ivy probably wanted to protect her daughter."

"And there's no way Elias Rivera would have married her if he knew about her child," Nat reasoned, leaning back in her chair. "Wow, poor Ivy. The more we find out about her, the more it makes me feel sorry for her."

"I don't think she would have wanted us to pity her," Charlotte said thoughtfully. "And you know, this makes a lot more sense. Now we know why she was so nervous about seeing Martin again."

Nat frowned, but her expression cleared as she realized what Charlotte was implying. "Ivy loved Martin," Nat said, gesturing to the photograph. "She was probably afraid to tell him that she had given their daughter up for adoption. Now I feel sorry for Martin. Do you think he really ran away?"

"It's hard to say," Charlotte said. "He was poor, and he had returned from the war a broken man. Maybe the news that his beloved Ivy was engaged to someone else and that she had given their baby up for adoption had pushed him over the edge. I hate to say it, but we can't rule out the possibility that he killed her."

"You have a point. Whoever put Ivy at the bottom of the well covered it up so that no one would find her. That either shows shame or an act of extreme rage. Maybe Martin was so angry with her that he killed her and dumped her body."

"Or if he lost his temper, maybe he hid what he had

done out of shame," Charlotte said. "I don't know a thing about him, but I still want to give him the benefit of the doubt. Is that weird?"

"No," Nat said, "after seeing that photo, I want to believe the best in him. Ivy certainly did. They didn't get a chance to be together, so I guess the next best thing is believing that their love was real. It would be even worse if Ivy spent all that time loving him only for him to murder her. I guess we're romantic that way."

"I never thought of myself as a romantic," Charlotte said in amusement.

"This case would be enough to bring out anyone's romantic side. I'm definitely not a romantic, but I'm still hoping for the best. Do you think we'll ever find out the truth, or is this one of those times when we have to fill in the blanks? Imagine being a historian; it would drive me crazy. I need facts and details."

"I think I'd enjoy being a historian," Charlotte said. "I think we need to find out what happened to baby Martina. I have a sneaking suspicion that it might be an important piece of the puzzle."

"I can use some of my connections to try and find out," Nat said.

As she spoke, Nat's phone chimed with a notification. She checked it, and her brow furrowed.

"What is it?" Charlotte asked.

"Look at this," Nat said, handing the phone to Charlotte. "They found this tucked into Annette's back pocket."

Charlotte squinted at the photo. It was a picture of an old piece of paper that had been folded into quarters. She immediately recognized Ivy's handwriting. After spending hours poring over Ivy's handwriting, it was becoming a familiar sight. Her eyes widened as she read the note.

Kingsley-

Martin's return has changed everything for me. I have given you control of my life, and it has led to my extreme unhappiness. I shall never forgive myself for giving my Martina up. While there is no doubt in my mind that you had my best interests at heart, I cannot ignore my conscience any longer. I will gladly give up all the money and status in the world to be with Martin.

I cannot ask you to agree with my choices, but I will ask you to respect them. This party is the last that I'll attend. Elias deserves to know the truth at the very least. Do not try to change my mind, I will be ending the engagement tonight, then Martin and I will be together at last. If you cannot be happy for me, then perhaps it is time that we parted ways.

-Ivy

"It looks like Ivy was finally standing up for herself," Nat said, raising her eyebrows.

"I wonder how Kingsley took the news," Charlotte said grimly.

CHAPTER FOURTEEN

*C*harlotte sat in front of the museum, trying to build up the courage to go back in. The police had removed all the tape from the door, and a cleaning crew had just left. It seemed to her that the police were done with the museum, but she was sure that something inside the building had gotten Annette killed.

After taking a few minutes to psych herself up, Charlotte got out of the car and hurried into the museum. The cleaning crew had left it unlocked, and Charlotte knew right away where she was heading. When she and Isla had spent the previous night going through the place, she had seen a room full of books and paperwork across from Annette's office.

Charlotte walked into the records' room and noted that the room smelled like old paper and mothballs. She took several deep breaths and reminded herself to breathe.

Every time she walked into the museum, she was transported to the moment when she had found Annette's body. It was an awful feeling, and no matter what she did, it was hard to move past it. Charlotte began looking through the records, when she realized that it was silly.

"If I'm right, and I hope that I am, then Annette would have been working on this when she died," Charlotte murmured to herself.

She walked out of the records' room and headed to the office. As she sat down, she began pulling out drawers and searching through them. When she didn't find anything, she leaned back in the chair and sighed in disappointment.

It was a comfortable adjustable leather chair that allowed a person to lean quite far back. Charlotte had had a similar chair back when she worked in an office. It was the only thing she missed from her days in an office environment.

The office chair creaked slightly, then stopped. Charlotte tried to lean further back in the swivel chair, but it wouldn't move. She frowned and looked under the chair curiously. To her surprise, a yellow envelope was taped to the bottom of the chair and had been blocking the chair from leaning further back.

"Bingo!" Charlotte said triumphantly as she pulled the envelope out.

She opened it to reveal a yellowing document. As she read through it, a bubble of relief swelled in her chest. When she had gotten to the museum, she hadn't known what she was looking for, but she knew that there had to be something.

The police seemed to be treating Annette and Ivy's murders as separate events, but she knew that they were connected. It seemed highly improbable that the two women would have anything in common since they were separated by an entire century, but it turned out that they had more in common than anyone could have imagined.

"Ivy was full of secrets," Charlotte said to herself as she took a picture of the document and sent it through to Nat.

Within a few moments, Nat called her.

"Does this mean what I think it does?" Nat asked, her tone tinged with excitement.

"I think so," Charlotte said. "I think I know who killed Annette, and I think I know why. Have your contacts gotten back to you yet?"

"Yes, thankfully Ivy gave birth in a private hospital

which kept amazing records. We have records for the Baker family as well as Martina. It turns out that Martina Baker married Ted Holmes. They gave birth to three children, one of whom was named Isabelle. Well, Isabella grew up and married Harris Thompson, and they had two children. Their daughter was named Claire and she married Winston Pass. And they gave birth to, you guessed it, none other than Annette Pass."

Charlotte listened intently as she folded the envelope precisely and slid it into her back pocket. She nodded as Nat spoke even though her friend couldn't see her. When she had seen the picture of Martina, she had been reminded of how familiar Ivy had looked to her. Then when it became apparent that Ivy had given up her daughter for adoption, it occurred to Charlotte that Ivy might have more relatives out there.

Everything had clicked as she saw the miniature portrait of Ivy in the museum. Ivy and Annette had similar facial features. Not enough to make their connection immediately apparent, but just enough for Charlotte to make the link.

It suddenly made sense why Annette had been so insistent about finding out everything about Ivy. Something Kenan had said also came back to Charlotte. He had mentioned that Annette made him feel embarrassed for not giving her every piece of his family's history. Her actions had struck many as entitled. It made perfect sense since Annette had in fact been entitled to every piece of Ivy's history.

"This is crazy," Charlotte breathed. "I can't believe we know what happened now."

As she spoke, she heard the floorboards creaking somewhere behind her. Charlotte's heart began beating quicker, and she walked carefully to the main room. There, Kenan Stanhope stood with a confused expression.

"Uh...I need to go," Charlotte said.

"What's going on?" Nat asked, but Charlotte didn't say anything and slipped her phone into her pocket.

"Oh," Kenan said in surprise. "I didn't know anyone was here. I'm so sorry."

Charlotte's skin went ice-cold, and she faked a pleasant smile. He looked unassuming, as if there was nothing wrong with sneaking into a museum that doubled as a crime scene.

"Hi, Kenan," Charlotte said, slightly breathlessly. "I'm sorry, I shouldn't be here either. You see, I decided to give up on this whole Ivy thing. It was silly of me to try. I'm sorry, I know you were hoping that I would find out what happened to her."

The relief on his face was evident, but he nodded slowly. "I understand. You're right, I would have liked to know what happened to her. It sounds stupid, but I think it would have been nice to finally put that whole chapter of my family's history to rest. I know how strange that sounds."

He laughed, and it sounded strange to Charlotte's ears. Her palms were sweaty, and she fought the urge to wipe them down the front of her jeans. The last thing she wanted was for him to know how nervous she was.

"It doesn't sound strange," Charlotte said gently. "I've seen how much this all means to you. This whole place is basically a monument to your family. If it weren't for the Stanhopes, then this town probably wouldn't be here."

She hoped that he would be swayed by the flattery. He seemed like the type of person who put a lot of stock in family and status. When his chest swelled with pride, she knew that she had been right. Charlotte was careful not to get too hopeful about his reaction. Things could change in an instant, and she didn't want to be caught off guard.

"Some people don't think that way," Kenan said with a sigh. "They think that the Stanhopes are a part of the past. Take Annette, for example. She was obsessed with this place. It made her stick her nose in where it didn't belong."

"There's a fine line between respecting someone's

history and stalking," Charlotte said simply. "Annette's death was a wakeup call for me. Knowing what happened in the past shouldn't come at the cost of the living."

Kenan's eyes brightened, and she allowed herself a small smile which he reciprocated.

"I'm so glad that you see it that way," Kenan said. "I didn't want to say anything, but I was beginning to get worried that you would blur the line too."

Charlotte took a step closer and looked down at the floor. She noticed a fleck of red paint on his shoes and felt a surprising fury rush through her. He hadn't even changed his shoes. That's how sure he was that he wouldn't be caught. It took all of her self-control to keep the pleasant smile fixed on her face.

"You never did tell me what you were doing here, though," Kenan said, and Charlotte froze again.

"Annette lent me a few of Ivy's things, and I thought it would be best if I brought them back," Charlotte said with a shrug. She was surprised by how quickly the lie rolled off her tongue. "I want to be done with all of this. I guess we'll never know what happened to Ivy. Maybe Martin killed her after all."

Kenan shrugged. "People don't like to think about it, but there's a reason why it's not good for people from different social backgrounds to mix. Poor Ivy found that out the hard way."

"It's a shame," Charlotte said with a forced smile. "Well, it's been nice seeing you, Kenan. I'll see you around."

She wanted to walk out the other door, but if she did that then he might have become suspicious. Instead, she moved casually past him. When she got close to the door, she felt a burst of hope but then he spoke.

"You never asked what I was doing here," Kenan said, causing her to turn and look at him.

His pale eyes regarded her coolly, and she glanced down at his hands. Those were the hands he had used to kill Annette. She had no doubt that he would likely use them on her.

"This place is full of your stuff," Charlotte said with a frown. "I figured that you probably came to pick something up."

Kenan's shoulders relaxed, and he nodded. "You know, Charlotte, if you ever find anything about Ivy or the Stanhopes, come to me first. I'd be happy to show my gratitude with a monetary reward. I'm sure that a woman like you can be counted on for her discretion."

Charlotte nodded at him. "I completely understand."

With that, she slipped out the door and exhaled in

relief. She took her phone out of her pocket and put it to her ear.

"Did you hear that?" Charlotte asked breathlessly.

"You handled that beautifully," Nat said gently. "I called the police as soon as I heard what was going on. They're on their way now."

"I don't think Ron will be able to handle this kind of thing," Charlotte said bitterly as she walked quickly to her car. "He might let Kenan off with a warning or something."

"No," Nat said heavily, "I called Brandon's cell. He promised that he's on his way now. You're going to be okay, Charlotte."

Charlotte wanted to cry in relief as she got in her car and stared at the museum. She needed to know if Kenan tried to leave the building.

"Thank you," she said. "I know how hard that must have been for you."

"I would do anything for you," Nat said dismissively. "Now, sit tight. The police are coming."

A few minutes later, Brandon drove up to the museum. As they parked, Charlotte got out of her car and noticed that he had brought backup. Her eyes prickled as relief overwhelmed her. They were taking her seriously.

"Here," Charlotte said, walking up to him with the

document in her hand. "This is the last will and testament of Ivy's father. He stipulated in his will that his estate would go to Ivy, and if she had any children, the estate would automatically go to her child. It meant that when Ivy had a baby, Kingsley was going to be left with nothing. And according to the note found on Annette Pass, Ivy was planning on cutting Kingsley out of her family."

Brandon nodded seriously as he took the document.

"Nat filled me in," he said grimly. "Annette was actually Ivy's closest living relative."

"She must have found that document and realized that the entire Stanhope fortune actually belonged to her," Charlotte said. "I'm guessing that Kenan took the news about as well as Kingsley did."

"Thanks, Char," Brandon said, nodding at her. "We appreciate the help. Come on, guys, let's go catch a murderer."

CHAPTER FIFTEEN

*a*bout a week later, Charlotte was sitting on her porch enjoying the sunset when Isla walked out of the house. Archimedes was lying in Charlotte's lap, and Roma was in the garden nearby trying to catch a locust.

"Okay, so I think that's it for today," Isla said. "I'll see you tomorrow."

"Wait," Charlotte said before Isla walked away. "Did I ever thank you for staying with me when everything was happening?"

Charlotte was feeling relaxed for the first time since she had moved to her grandmother's place. Now that she didn't have to try and solve two murders, she'd been taking stock of everything that had happened. One thing stood out for her, and that was the fact that she hadn't expressed nearly enough appreciation for Isla.

"You didn't need to," Isla said. "I know you'd do the same for me."

"I know, but I still want to thank you. I want you to know that you can tell me anything. You don't need to worry about how I might react."

Charlotte's heart jumped to her throat. It wasn't always easy for her to talk about her feelings. When she did, it heightened her anxiety. And she was nervous that if she brought the subject up, Isla might be forced to reveal that she was going to leave permanently. Charlotte couldn't picture living in her grandmother's house without Isla.

Isla frowned. "What's this about?"

"I heard you talking on the phone when I first got here," Charlotte admitted. "You were telling someone that you had something to tell me, and you weren't sure how you were going to say it."

Isla's brow scrunched further then she nodded with understanding. "I'm sorry about that. It's…well, to be honest, I didn't know how to say it so I just kind of thought that I wasn't going to say anything."

"What is it?" Charlotte asked in concern.

"Well," Isla said, twisting her hands nervously. "It's just that Jenny was very grateful for my service over the years, so she put some money aside for me. She wanted to make sure that I would always have a job here. So, she made it a condition of your inheritance that if you took the house then you would have to employ me. I didn't know if the lawyer had told you, and I didn't know how to bring it up without sounding conceited. Your grandmother just died and here I was worrying about my job."

Charlotte let out a heavy breath and smiled. She couldn't believe what she was hearing. It felt like a weight was being lifted off her shoulders. Isla wasn't leaving after all, and that made her almost giddy with happiness.

"You were worried about that?" Charlotte asked in amazement. "I thought you were getting ready to leave because there was no reason for you to stay now that my grandmother is gone."

"You're plenty of reason for me to stay," Isla said, looking touched by Charlotte's words.

Charlotte's eyes became misty, and she cleared her throat before assuming a more casual demeanor.

"And I knew about the stipulation in the will," Charlotte said with a shrug. "I thought it was fair, and I was happy that she had taken care of you. Even if she hadn't, I still would have wanted you to stay. You're like my family."

Isla touched her chest and beamed at Charlotte.

"Your grandmother would have been so proud of you. When she told me that she was leaving the house to you, I was worried that you wouldn't do well in this town. It can get claustrophobic sometimes, and I know you struggle with social situations, but look at you now! You're all famous."

Charlotte blushed. When the police had arrested Kenan, he had confessed to the crime. Apparently, he had left some trace evidence at the scene, and they had a strong case against him. Charlotte's evidence had been the nail in his coffin. However, the local newspaper made it seem like Charlotte solved the entire thing on her own.

As soon as Charlotte read the article, she had called the newspaper and told them to edit it. They printed an amendment to the article the next day to include that Charlotte had merely assisted the police department and that Isla, Nat, and Amy had helped a lot as well.

Nat had called to tell Charlotte that Amy was very impressed with them both, and they had been getting along better than ever. That news was enough to put Charlotte in a good mood for a month.

Two days after the story appeared, another bomb-shell was dropped. The police had searched the Stanhope Estate and had found Martin Baker's remains in the garden. He had been murdered around the same time as Ivy, which proved that he never abandoned his family or Ivy. It was a touching story, and several reporters had already called Charlotte to hear her side of the story. She didn't have any interest in telling them anything.

Her adventure had endeared her to the local towns-people, and several people had stopped by to introduce themselves. For the first time since she arrived, Charlotte felt as though she might have a future in the small town.

"I'm not famous," Charlotte scoffed. "All I did was find the truth. And I got lucky. Anyone could have done it."

"I don't know about that," Isla said dubiously. "Besides, no one else did it. You did. And I think it was very sweet of you to have my name included in the article."

"You deserved it," Charlotte insisted. "I mean, you snuck into the museum with me in the middle of the night. I don't know many people who would do that."

Isla laughed and shook her head. "Your craziness is rubbing off on me."

"Maybe it's your craziness that's rubbing off on me," Charlotte pointed out. "I never used to do this kind of thing before you came around, and now look."

"To be fair, I didn't do anything like this, either," Isla

said.

As she spoke, Charlotte spotted someone walking down her driveway. She frowned as she looked at him. He was tall and handsome with curly, sandy-brown hair and a square face. He had deep brown eyes and an easy smile. She tried to remember if she had met him before, but nothing came to mind.

As soon as she saw what was in his hands, everything snapped into place, and she scowled at him. Isla looked around in confusion and when she saw who was walking toward them, she smiled broadly.

"Hi," the man said with a nervous expression, "I'm Levi; I live next door."

Isla looked eagerly at Charlotte, as if to gauge her reaction. It looked like Isla was enjoying the show, and Charlotte glared at her. Isla merely shrugged her shoulders and smiled wider. Charlotte couldn't help but note that he had a quiet manner about him and a sweet sort of handsomeness. Her cheeks turned pink, and she struggled to meet his eyes. Finally, the reality of his introduction dawned on her, and she looked up in annoyance. All thoughts about his looks flew out of her head as she narrowed her eyes at him.

He took a step back in surprise.

"So, you're the one who's been trying to pawn that ugly thing off on me," Charlotte said, crossing her arms over her chest.

"In my defense, it is a truly ugly gnome," Levi said sheepishly. "And I never in my wildest dreams thought that it would escalate like it did."

Charlotte snorted, but she had to admit that he made sense. She hadn't thought it would escalate the way it had, either. His reasonable reply knocked some of the wind out of her sails. Before she could respond, Isla beat her to the punch.

"No worries, Levi," Isla said, waving her hand dismissively. "Do you want some lemonade? Are you single?"

"Isla!" Charlotte hissed, her cheeks turning red. "What are you doing?"

"He's cute, you're cute," Isla said with a shrug. "Okay, I'm going to get some lemonade."

With that, she walked into the house, leaving a mortified Charlotte behind.

"Please excuse her," Charlotte choked out. "I just told her she's like my family, so naturally she's determined to be the most embarrassing relative in existence."

"It makes sense," Levi said with a laugh. "You should see my aunts back home. Anytime a woman comes close, they try to marry me off. It got embarrassing, so I decided to come out here and start fresh."

His cheeks turned bright red, and Charlotte found his reaction endearing.

"It makes sense," Charlotte said with an amused smile. "So what do you do around here when you're not busy tormenting me with the gnome?"

"I'm a book antiquarian," Levi explained. "This area has some great history, and now that I'm down here permanently, I'm hoping to find some interesting specimens."

"You're in luck," Charlotte said excitedly. "My grandmother had an extensive collection which she left to me. Some of them were damaged in a flood, so I'm busy rebinding them. I think you might be able to find some treasures in there. I'm not looking to sell anything though, so don't get too excited."

"I'll keep that in mind," Levi said, looking amused. "And going back to the gnome, I really am sorry about everything. When the police came over a few nights ago, I thought for sure that you had called them on me. In my mind, it was just a few harmless pranks. I never thought that you'd be so offended."

"I didn't call the cops on you," Charlotte said primly.

"I know that now. I wanted to come over and apologize the next day, but you weren't around. Now I know why. I read about what you did in the paper; that was impressive."

"Thanks," Charlotte said, her cheeks turning red. "I was only trying to find out what happened to Ivy because I found her. I felt like I owed it to her, you know?"

"I can't say that I relate but I admire your tenacity," Levi said with a smile. "I can't believe how it all worked out in the end. And we had fun along the way. Well, I thought it was fun," he said simply. "You know, I told my mom about it, and she told me that I needed to get a hobby?"

"Gnome swapping is kind of like a hobby," Charlotte said in amusement.

"She does not agree," Levi said, pretending to be serious. "She demanded that I come back home before I embarrass her any further."

Charlotte chuckled.

"You know, I've been thinking," Levi said, scratching the back of his neck awkwardly. "Maybe we could spend some time together. I think we could have some fun."

It sounded like a line that a womanizer would use, but he looked so flustered when he said it that Charlotte's heart melted a little.

"Sure, I think that sounds great," Charlotte said, "and maybe in the meantime we could share custody of the world's ugliest gnome."

Levi beamed happily. "Sure, that sounds like a plan."

# # #

Thank you for reading! Want to help out?

Reviews are crucial for independent authors like me, so if you enjoyed my book, **please consider leaving a review today**.

Thank you!

Penny Brooke

ABOUT THE AUTHOR

Penny Brooke has been reading mysteries for as long as she can remember. When not penning her own stories, she enjoys spending time outdoors with her husband, crocheting, and cozying up with her pups and a good novel. To find out more about her books, visit www.pennybrooke.com

Made in the USA
Las Vegas, NV
30 April 2024